SOOR HEARTS

Soor Hearts

Robert Alan Jamieson

Paul Harris Publishing
Edinburgh

First published 1983 by
Paul Harris Publishing,
40 York Place,
Edinburgh

ISBN 0 86228 072 9

The Publishers gratefully acknowledge the financial assistance
of the Scottish Arts Council in the publication of this book

Printed in Scotland by
The Shetland Times Ltd., Prince Alfred Street, Lerwick, Shetland

For Wilma

Since completing this short yarn, my thoughts have wandered to the usage of the Shetland dialect in this work, and I have arrived at the conclusion that this subject is worth a little explanation.

I may be accused of having bastardised what may have been a then very definite dialect. In defence, I would point out that my intention was always to write a tale which would flow, and would to some extent bring the past alive, and I felt that over-expression of the idiosyncratic nature of the dialect might in some way affect my chances of succeeding. Therefore, I have used dialect in a form which I feel is easily readable and still preserves, I feel, the particular nature and qualilties of Shetlandic.

Should I offend the purists, may they forgive me. I too love my culture, and that is the reason why I choose to write of it.

I would like to express my thanks to John J. Graham and Basil Wishart for their help and guidance.

Robert Alan Jamieson,

Melby,
Sandness.
April, 1983.

Chapter One

Hamefarin'

The sky and sea had fused; one intruding on the others' province. Sketched in the mists, with minimal detail, a small steamer, puffing smoke, a darker grey imposed upon the formless mists, rounded the skerries which lay off Crugness, and anchored in the mouth of Mirkwick.

A boat set out from the small pier to meet the steamer, unable to come into the bay itself because of the shallows. At the pierhead many of the villagers had set aside their labours to attend, expectantly chewing over the weather, but all waiting for more interesting topics to emerge from the mouths of the disembarking passengers.

These mornings were unproductive in terms of work, but none the less vital to the social balance of the village for that, being the time when the news from the rest of the islands, and farther afield, finally filtered through to the eager ears waiting at the quayside.

Titbits to be masticated by the fishermen mending their nets, by the women stopping at the well to pass a few minutes. Varied information, its truth often chequered, dependent on the number of mouths it had passed through since action had given birth to it. Yet always vital. Tongues without gossip talked anyway, and those hollow mouthings were far more malicious than the harmless discussion of external topics. The state of the herring season. The price of commodities in Lerwick. The same subjects in the alehouse, by the quayside, at the well, by the fireside. But always tossed about with fresh interest, animated.

Today saw the return of the laird's son from his school in Edinburgh. He was virtually a stranger to the people of the village, a frail boy of eighteen, whose life was a thin line strung between the isolation of his boyhood, and the intense action of his future. Two rough hands reached up to him as he gingerly stepped into the boat, but he preferred to reach out and grasp the tarry ropes for assistance. The boy extended no greeting to the sailors but positioned himself in the stern and glared as his luggage — a large trunk and expensive looking valise — followed him into the flit boat.

The oarsmen began to row ashore, though the boat could have held more cargo. Their strokes were long and powerful, eloquent even, in a wordless way. The boy gazed out to the hidden horizon, his blonde curls wisping over the collar of a dark emerald velvet jacket. The whole experience of coming into contact with the seamen was profoundly displeasing to him. Yet there was no other way to reach the safety of his father's carriage, waiting, baroque and stylish, powered by two immaculate grey mares, their tails held high.

At the small pier, the boy was assisted ashore by the grieve, who had brought the carriage to meet him, although it was only a matter of a hundred yards or so to the Haa House, which stood vast and gloomy by the shore, surrounded by huge walled gardens hiding the ground floor from peasant eyes. He shook the boy's hand warmly, and shouted at the oarsman to be careful with the luggage. The welcoming smile and the expression of irritation shown to the seaman so contrasted one another that it was obvious to all who watched that neither were sincere.

The flit boat returned to the steamer side. Four more passengers alighted: Mr and Mrs Williamson, the local merchant and his wife, returned from their yearly visit to her cousin in Lerwick; a young girl of middle teens, that none recognised, and lastly, a red haired man, with wild uncontrollable beard, a seaman, judging by the tattoos on his forearms. He carried a rough canvas kitbag, of the type sailors used.

"Whit news fae Lerwick, Mr Williamson? And did you have a fine time?"

People pushed forward goodnaturedly, firing questions at the travellers, who made no attempt to answer. Mr Williamson, a rotund fellow of middle age, with a great handle-bar moustache which he waxed regularly, smiled. His forehead was broad with lines of concentration which had been moulded over accounts and ledgers. It was a task that had never come easily to him. The business had been his fathers, and he had inherited it, book-keeping and all.

Mrs Williamson winced uncomfortably, amid all the attention given to her. Her eyes twitched nervously, secretly wishing for the safety of her own little house next to the shop. In those surroundings her nervousness would disappear, and she would regale her rather plain self with all the airs and graces of a lady, entertaining those whom she considered her equals socially. She would spread her idea of the local concerns in an affected accent known in dialect as "knapin' ". Folk berated her snobbery. She had little to be so proud of, herself a daughter of Bob o da Neap, a light fingered old de'il, that might take the very peat from your fire, given the chance. But like so many her snobbery was rooted in self-conciousness. Night often met her sleepless, so troubled was she by the impression she may or may not have given so and so.

At this moment, a great rattle and spitting of stones from under wheels occurred, and the laird's carriage returned to the pierhead, the grey mares stepping out under the lash of a thin whip held by the grieve. The laird himself rested in the back, stone-faced, looking neither to the right or the left. The crowd split open to allow him to pass, as if themselves struck by the same thin whip. The carriage stopped where the young girl passenger stood, watching the commotion caused by the merchant and his wife. The laird did not move a muscle, excepting those of his eyes, which ran over the girl's body like rats, exploring even the hidden parts of her figure.

At last, when the red had flushed to her cheeks and her eyes were fixed on the ground before her, he spoke.

"Ellen Mitchell?"

"Yessir," she curtseyed.

"You're very young, aren't you?"

"Sixteen, sir, though I'll be seventeen this winter."

Another silence during which scrutiny continued.

"Well, come along girl," he bellowed, when he had tired of his game of humiliation.

The girl, still not able to look at the landowner, stooped to pick up her single suitcase, to find to her horror that it sprang open and emptied half it's contents over the cobbles.

"Good Lord, girl, are you always so clumsy?" he shouted again.

"No sir." Her hands shook as she stuffed her most personal belongings back into the suitcase, her spirit broken in the knowledge that half the village had examined her undergarments. Face puckered for weeping, she climbed into the carriage beside the laird, still averting her eyes from his. She sat in the very corner, as if desiring not to be in the carriage at all. The grieve cracked his whip, and the horses leapt into action, horseshoes clopping cobblestones. Laughter broke out among the young men in attendance, humorous comments tossed about. Among the rest, a bubbling of curiosity arose.

Mrs Williamson cracked her silent mouth.

"She's to be the lady's companion. From Edinburgh," she said, almost in a whisper, and then immediately regretted having spoken, as this piece of news had been the one she wished to savour most.

The best bits of gossip brought home from her yearly trip to Lerwick, she kept for a few days, glowering over them in her mind, like a bairn treasuring the Christmas sugar pig until Easter. She would unwrap it in her mind and play with it, this titbit, mulling over whether the time was ripe to share it. She might or might not. It was her secret, and this was what made it so much fun for her. Gossip was her escape from routine family life, her hobby in a way, though were you to call it gossip to her face, she would have been deeply affronted. To her, it was just a little pleasure. Everyone has at least one vice, she would tell herself as she combed her now greying locks in the mirror, sighing at Time's harshness.

The Williamsons had two daughters, Agnes and Mary. Neither was married and they remained at home in the house next the shop. They had been well provided for, and groomed by Mrs Williamson to the point where none of the men of the parish were really suitable, bar the factor and the minister. Mary, the elder, was at present being courted by the minister, the Reverend William Cunningham, from St Andrews. Word had it that he was too old for her, and that their match would be a mistake, but in truth there was only ten years between them. He looked much older than his thirty-six years, and she was now well past the usual age for a girl to wed. There wasn't much love between them. For his part, he felt that he needed a wife to enhance his social position, and perhaps assist his career in the ministry. Mary Williamson was not the type to care too much for love. She was practical and intelligent — and dangerously near spinsterhood.

Agnes, the younger daughter, and the more charming, was her mother's favourite. She played upon this to gain everything she wanted. They were very close, Agnes and her mother, in all but their attitudes to marriage. Agnes was accomplished with embroidery needle, played the piano passably, and contrived the daintiest watercolours with her slender hand. Mrs Williamson felt she displayed all the qualities that constitute breeding, and sent her to her cousin's for the winter in the hope that she might find a suitable young man. But Agnes had returned by herself, and explained that she had no interest in men. She had time for only one member of the opposite sex — young Peter Jacobsen, who worked for her father in the shop. And this was because they shared an interest in what Agnes called the finer things of life — Art and Music. Her mother took this disclosure badly. Peter was a fine enough lad, but Agnes could do much better. An armed truce persisted.

Mrs Williamson's reverie was broken by the sound of her husband laughing at the "Sooth lasses drawers", as Aald Seemon Sinclair a' Breck had put it. She kicked him slyly on the ankle, and gestured to the shop. Together, they entered, leaving the crowd outside still grinning and guffawing . . .

The fourth passenger on the steamer that day had taken advantage of the merriment to slip unnoticed into the alehouse at the pierhead. Only Aald Seemon saw him go. In his sharp old head, a memory stirred, but he couldn't place it.

Haakie Manson, the white-aproned red nosed proprietor of the Böd, sang out a greeting.

"Goodday to you sir. A stranger, I believe, and a sailor too, by da look of it . . ."

He was practised at sudden summations of people. It was *his* hobby. A man's dress, the cut of his hair, the look in his eye. Haakie put it together into a pattern in an instant. And, though he said it himself, he wasn't often wrong.

The stranger didn't reply. He came down the two stone steps into the tiny tavern, and put his kit bag on a seat. With his back to the light, his face was shadowed. A sudden irrational wave of intuition ran down Haakie's spine.

"Whit'll it be? A drop of rum for a sailor's mouth?" suggested Haakie. No reply. The sailor sat down alongside his bag.

"Come along, sir, I don't have time for games," the proprietor continued.

"I'll have dat gold sovereign du owns me, Haakie Manson . . ."

Haakie ran through his memories. A door opened, and the stranger's identity slumped out like a corpse.

"Magnus!"

"Aye, it's me, right enough."

"Whit brings dee back here?" he asked guardedly.

The sailor smiled, his head suddenly catching the light from a small side window, illuminating a face weathered and scarred, a nose broken and crookedly sharp. Eyes burned blue under a protruding forehead, deep set.

"Oh, deevilment, Haakie. As ever, deevilment," the red beard shook. But his voice carried no commitment. Haakie poured two glasses of rum and went to the front door, which he shut and bolted.

"I'll close dis," he said, and returned to Magnus' side, where he sat down.

In the dark of the tavern, the two men raised their glasses silently.

"Whit is it, ten years?" said Haakie.

"Not far off," replied Magnus, sipping from his glass. "Sometimes it seems a whole lifetime, though . . ."

Haakie mopped his forehead with a soiled handkerchief, and stuffed it back in his pocket. His face was red and round, his head bald. He liked to know everything that went on, and here in the alehouse, there wasn't much that he couldn't learn about the goings-on in the parish. People came and went. He met all kinds, from the factor to the poorest crofter. He spoke with them all, and so had a wide knowledge of other people's affairs. He would hear both sides of every disagreement, and side with both, for that was how he learnt most.

"I'm not sure if du's brave or foolish, Magnus," he said, "but wan way or anidder, dey'll be an awful uproar, ten years or no'."

Magnus ran his fingers through his mop of wiry red hair . . .

"So I'm no' forgotten in Mirkwick, dan?"

He filled and lit his pipe. The smoke wisped upward in a blue aromatic mist through the shafts of light from the window. The air in the alehouse was poised with a chill expectancy, as Haakie Manson sensed himself on the edge of a scoop. Magnus Doull's return! He had never expected it. The gold sovereign he'd wagered against Doull ever returning to Mirkwick, that moonlit night almost a decade ago, had seemed secure in his publican's pocket. Yet he was pleased to have lost this bet. The news of Doull's would be worth a sovereign and more.

"Whit brings dee back?" he repeated his original question.

Magnus sucked on his pipe, shrugged. Why had he come back?

"A few reasons, Haakie. No wan thing. I wis nineteen and scared when I left. I didna ken whit I wis doing. I wis running fast, and never thought whit I wis running towards. No man can run awa' aa' his life . . ."

"Conscience," asserted Haakie Manson.

"No, man, not conscience. If I did wrong, I did it without kenning. I ran fae da unknown."

He looked oddly at the glass of rum before him.

"Du canna ken whit torture dat is. No man can."

The publican's face screwed up into an expression of concentration. A minute passed, silent.

"So du's here to bide?" he asked.

"Bide? Wha kens?"

The sailor clicked his boot heels on the stone floor, rhythmically. Haakie sipped his rum. There was so much he wanted to find out from Doull, too much almost, for he didn't want to chase him away by being too eager.

"And whar's du been all dis years, Magnus?" he began cautiously, fishing for an opening into real conversation.

"Been? Whar have I been? A thousand different Hells, Haakie, in a thousand different ports the world over. I'm a merchant seaman noo. At least, I wis."

The obtuse nature of his conversation annoyed the publican. He wanted information. Doull seemed very distracted, unlike the headstrong young man Haakie had helped escape the hands of the law ten years before. The fire had passed out of him. He was old enough to know the troubles and the puzzles of past mistakes.

"I've been drunk from Valparaiso to Vladivostock. I've had hoors fae every continent."

The rum loosened his thoughts, and linked them better to the tongue. Magnus' mind ran back through the years. It all seemed as if it had never happened.

"A waste, Haakie. I should never have listened ta dee. I should have stayed and faced da truth. I'd rather have died a murderer on the gallows."

Unexpectedly, he asked a question of his own.

"Tell me, is my midder still livin'?" A second of dread so tight gripped him that his knuckles whitened where they held his glass.

"Ja," said Haakie. "She's da sam as ever. She keeps hersel' ta hersel'. We see little of her here."

Relief exhaled from the sailor's lips. He pictured her in his imagination: one-eyed, shrewd, steeped in the mysteries of the past and the future. A thin lip of skin curling over the dead eye, her face charted by the lines of age.

"Whit'll du do for work?" asked Haakie, finding space for a question.

Magnus opened the kitbag by his side. He held its canvas mouth open for a mere second, yet it was enough for Haakie to see the banknotes inside. His greedy eyes swelled wide and hungry.

"But how?" he began, popeyed.

"Gun-runnin' . . ." But no more than that was he willing to divulge.

Haakie pryed for more information, but Magnus staved off his attempts skillfully. He had need of information himself. Ten years bring many changes that often go unobserved by those who live through them, but to the exile, they are so abrupt that they represent a destruction sudden and unsympathetic. Magnus desired this diluted by Haakie's knowledge. His head was full of the doings of the parish. Minutely detailed accounts passed through his ears to the store in his mind. He could tell Magnus everything he wanted to know and more.

"So du thinks da past will be dug up, noo I'm back, Haakie? Dey'll no' let it lie?"

"Ach, Magnus, dey'll be dem that'll no' rest till du's tried. How can it be idder? It wis a murder, an unsolved murder at dat. It took a lang time for da scandal ta die doon. Dere's some dat have never let it die. His wife, or widow, for wan."

Haakie fetched the bottle from the counter, and filled both glasses brimful, so they had to put their lips to the glass to avoid spillage as they raised them.

"And whar is she noo?"

"She has a room let at da back o' da Böd. Abön wan o' da stores. She gets something for cleaning and cooking at da manse, and she maks. She never married again. Her head is grey though she's barely thirty. She'll react badly when she hears du's back."

Magnus struck another match, to light the pipe which had gone out.

"I'm no' here ta cause trouble, Haakie. I still have no recollection of dat night, whar I wis or what I did. I can't believe I killed him, yet I can't be sure I didna. I'd like ta ken myself da truth of dat night. But I don't want any more battles. It's not really in my hands, Haakie. Something forced me back here, something I canna understand. It's purpose is beyond me.''

Haakie got up from the table, and went across to the small side window. It looked out on the shore line, where the sea, grey and lifeless, swelled slow and melodiously over the pebbly beach. Drift decorated the tideline, bits of dead seaweed, sea-worn wood, all brought to this place by mysterious combinations of tides and fates, through no decision of its own. Magnus Doull was drift. Life threw him up on beaches as it chose. Now it had brought him back to Mirkwick.

And there would be trouble.

Mirkwick. Strips of cultivated land, and tiny stone-built houses huddled into sparse shelter provided by the undulating plain. Each house the vessel of grains of life, a family, each with a story reaching back to the man whose hands had hewn the stone and laid the blocks together with mortar in the seams. Houses that held hopes fast in their walls, houses that had observed misery and illness, that had seen life evaporate with the peat smoke through the hole in the thatched roof. And houses that knew the joy of children content in the security of family.

Mirkwick. The boats dotted along the shoreline of the stony beach. Boats that bobbed in a sea of chance, that carried the men to the fishing grounds forty miles away over open seas. That carried the fragments of human life, dipped in the mystique of superstition, with a code of behaviour distinctly defined; words that could not be spoken, items that epitomised evil luck.

Mirkwick. Men and women squeezing out a basic existence from tired soil and cruel sea, prey to the whims of Nature. Prey to the consumption, hiding in the walls of the house, waiting, in the clothes of Father passed to the eldest son so as not to waste.

When they laid him into his grave, and the funeral was done with, Mary of Myres took her son by the hand and led him to the door of the crofthouse. She opened it on a fine summer's night and, with tears in her eyes, she spoke to him softly of the future and of what was expected of him. He was fourteen then. The family was eight. Johnsons, fatherless, little dirty faces peering out of the lamplight, where the peat smoke swirled and flowed slowly upward through the rafters. The consumption, the slow wasting killer, hiding in the gloom. The Johnsons sat round the fire that night, while she read to them from the family Bible. The children's eyes filled with awe, and tears, for Faither was gone, the coffin lifted from the ben room where it had lain with his face blue to whiteness, and his stare gone, eyes impressionless.

He rose from his bed that night, without waking his sleeping brothers. He crept through the house. He opened the doors silently, his feet touching the cold stone floor, and fumbled in the dark until he found the musty cloth. He put the jacket round his shoulders, shoved his arms through the sleeveholes, and the garment hung loose on him. He fought tears. He was the eldest now, the man of the house, and he would act like it. He would work and the work would fill out his lean shape. The coat would fit him soon . . .

"Ollie Johnson's dead," said Haakie suddenly. "The consumption like his Faither. Three weeks ago it wis."

He turned away from the window.

"He wis a good friend a' dine, wis he no'?"

"Magnus?"

The alehouse was deserted. Magnus Doull had taken his kitbag, and slipped out the door while Haakie was gazing out the window. Haakie took the empty glasses from the table.

"Aye, dere'll be trouble aricht," he muttered.

He put the glasses on the counter and went to the door. He saw Magnus, his red hair plainly identifiable, striding out towards the croft of Turmtillen, where his mother lived, alone with her potions and her remedies, and God kens whit else.

The rum in Haakie's mouth had a sour taste.

He closed the door from the outside, put a great iron key in the lock and turned it. He put the key in his apron pocket, and set out on foot. He had business in mind.

Chapter Two

Soor Hearts, Bitter Wishes

The widow Pole lived alone in a small house down by the pierhead. She lived on the top floor, and the ground floor was used by some of the fishermen as a store. A flight of stone steps by the side of the building led up to the front door. She had only one room, furnished in meagre fashion — a broken chair, an old table, and her organ.

She cleaned and cooked for the Reverend Cunningham at the Manse, and for her needs sold her knitting to Robert Williamson. There was no comfort in her life save her religion. It was her solace, and was all she needed. The tragedy of her Thomas was so imprinted on her mind that she had no room for anything else.

Her hair had greyed prematurely. Although her face remained youthful at thirty two, she seemed much older because of her hair, and her manner. She had the sympathy of the parish. It was hard on her, aa'body agreed, first her being barren and all, and then to have her husband torn from her by that cruel hand.

Her life was a solitary one; she kept her little home scrubbed clean, and saw few folk. The minister, Haakie Manson, her neighbour, and, much to her displeasure, Nina, the sailors' whore who lived in a similar dwelling by the shore.

It was strange the fate that had bound these two

women together. Nina, fat and sensual, the widowed Isabella thin and sour, living side by side, never exchanging a word.

Isabella Agnes, yearning for a murdered man, up all night in the paraffin light, with her patched clothes, and her spindly hands, clawing and pumping at the squeaky old organ, her prized possession and window to God. Isabella Agnes, consecrated, she wears only black of the deepest shade. She lives in a vacuum, of words never spoken, never releases her terrible hate.

Nina the comforter, a sip from the bottle, lies half awake for the sound of the latch. A regular caller, a man of the ocean, who swaggers in drunken with a mouthful of hate. She takes what they give her, not cheapened or begging, she delivers their passions, eases their ache.

They have both known ill luck. They have both felt the tiny daggers of loss turn and twist inside them, drawing blood till the very soul shrivels and knows no feeling.

But Isabella Agnes had maintained the respect of the community after her loss by stringing a rope of mournful dedication to walk along. Nina, in the time of her life, a whale of a girl, had given up the secrets she kept for one ear to many; she had become a woman of easy virtue. That dark night, the first, the straw in the byre, the stamping of the aald coo's hoof in the squelch of her stall, the rustling of cloth, his breath making clouds in the frosty air hot and impatient, her curls uncurled, secrets told, and then the awful consequence.

Not that she cared. There had only ever been one for her, in the same manner as Isabella treasured one heart. They were not so different, these two neighbours who never spoke.

One expressed her sorrow in the repression of pleasureable impulses, the other in their explosion, but the root cause was the same — the same man. The man who had given to Nina had taken from Isabella Agnes

Pole, and in so doing he was lost to the heart of the prostitute forever. Magnus Doull, murderer for one, lost love for the other.

Rock of Ages cleft for me, let me hide myself in thee. She polishes her faith as she polishes her shoes, to hide the scuff marks of the hatred she bears for the man who is her devil. Magnus Doull.

While Nina combs her brown curls, and paints the rouge on her cheeks, and kisses the photograph of *the* man, her first. The one she loves. Magnus Doull.

A figure scuttled along through the half-dark that night about nine o' clock. A sailor perhaps, on his way to visit Nina?

He was clad in a long ragged coat, and dragged one leg awkwardly behind the other. He mounted the steps to Nina's door, stepping up, then lifting the other leg with an effort. He was a small man, with dark hair and swarthy complexion. He knocked on the door.

Nina was entertaining a Dutchman. She heard the knock, and made her apologies to her guest, who swore at the interruption in his own language. Nina opened the door. She saw the figure of Creepin' Ertie, the cripple, tugging at his forelock.

A few words were exchanged, in whispers. The light illuminated the dark visage of the caller; jet black hair, small eyes.

The sailor heard Nina close the door, and she returned to him smiling. He poured from the bottle he had brought, into a chipped cup, and he drank. Then throwing the cup aside, he grabbed the flabby waist of the comforter and hauled her onto the bed beside him. The sound of the cripple's awkward step snap-shuffled down the steps.

Nina kissed the strange lips, inhaled the smell of the rum from his breath. A faraway look entered her gaze.

She listened to the steps of the cripple over the cobbles grow more and more distant . . .

Creepin' Ertie had been shipwrecked on the reefs beyond Crugness many years ago. He was the sole survivor of his crew, washed ashore amid the broken timber and the tang, found by Aald Seemon a' Breck, with his leg so badly fractured that the bones poked splintered from the flesh. Bessie, Seemon's wife, had nursed him. He was only a lad of fifteen then.

The leg healed, but crooked. He carried it behind him as if it was manacled, and this had given rise to his name. He had been christened Arturo, and was Italian. So Creepin' Ertie stuck.

Ertie was a part of Mirkwick. He was old, nobody knew how old, and he seemed one of them in a way. He found work in the smithy, sweeping up and the like. Andrew the blacksmith let him sleep in the loft above the workshop. He was a willing worker, despite his disability, and a man of honour. As long as he could remember, there had been those who abused him, but he didn't mind that. He had his friends. Friends who respected him for his trustworthy nature, and who used him as a messenger, knowing that any secret would be safe with him. He could often be seen, roaming from one house to another when his work at the smithy was over. He might earn a penny or two in this means and was able to avoid begging. Sometimes Isabella would bring him a bruinie fresh from the griddle, or Seemon might give him some fish.

He hobbled over the pierhead to the alehouse, his slow ungainly stride step-drag-step-drag.

As he opened the door, the hot air rushing out overcame him. The pub was busy.

People laughed as he entered.

"Aye, aye, here's Cripple Ertie . . . "

"Good evenin . . . ," he answered their jeers politely.

He hirpled forward to the bar, through a crowd of fishermen swilling ale. A hand grabbed him by the shoulder, arresting his progress.

"Dancing da night, Ertie?"

A large drunken fishermen squeezed his shoulder till it hurt. The others in his company laughed.

"Or is du courtin' Isabella?" another grinned.

Arturo wriggled out of the fisherman's grip, and turned to Haakie who had been laughing with the crew.

Haakie said something to the cripple which was lost in the general hub-bub. The head nodded, and Haakie went back to his customers.

"When's du gaain' ta git some decent claes, Ertie?," the fisherman continued. Arturo merely smiled politely, and started to leave. Again the heavy hand on his shoulder.

"Bide a while, Ertie, hae a dram."

The hand gripped him tighter.

"No . . . I . . ."

"Whit? Did I hear him say *'No'*, boys?"

The crew closed in on the poor cripple, encircling him, all ablaze with whisky and rum. They roared and laughed as the leader poured his beer over the cripple's head, then spun him round by his shoulders.

"Have a drink noo, Ertie?"

On dizzy legs, with awkward stance, Arturo fell over into a pool of beer.

"No, I can't. It makes me sick," he said from the floor.

Suddenly a fist landed on the chin of the antagonist, sending him crashing back on to the bar. Talking stopped.

A huge Dutchman from the ship moored in the mouth of Mirkwick, backed by three of his crewmates, stood in the midst of the fishermen.

"You leave him," said the Dutchman, "or I kill you."

Haakie Manson tried to intervene, but they shoved him out of the way. The two men faced up to each other angrily, squaring for a fight. The fishermen rubbed his face where the blow had landed. The Dutchman, six foot six at the very least, was a bit too big. But outside, later, with surprise on their side, it might be different.

Arturo made his escape while he could, leaving the knife-edge atmosphere inside for the calm of the cool night air. How he hated going into that place! Yet often Haakie would send for him, with a message to deliver, and he had no choice but to go, for Haakie sometimes gave him a penny for his services. That was a lot of money for the cripple.

He began to walk home to his bed in the loft at the smithy. He passed the shop and the factor's house, and his eye was caught by the shade of a figure against the lamplight, closing the curtains. For a minute, he thought it was a woman, but, no, it couldn't have been. The factor was an honourable man like Arturo himself.

He stopped by the steps that led up to Nina's house. It was cold, and his coat no longer kept out the chill as it once had done. Nina had given him that coat. It had been left behind by one of her gentlemen. But she had given it to him! To Arturo! Yes, and he is a cripple.

The wind in the alleys between the houses of the shore whistled as the breeze picked up and blew inshore from the open sea. The moon above rose pale and new, its outline crisp and well defined. Stars appeared and disappeared in the sky, shining then dying away, then shining again.

Creepin' Ertie began to walk once more over the cobbles, tapping and shuffling till the cobbles ended at the Haa, and only a gutter track went on. Nina, awake in the arms of her nameless sailor, heard him go by. She heard him stop outside, and pictured his dark-featured face. She did not trust Arturo. Sometimes, when he looked at her, it was with something concealed. He was not open with her, as most men were, either in their disgust or their desire. A whore is a whore, for some an angel, for others a devil. Arturo saw Nina as neither, and she sensed it.

He reached the smithy, and climbed slowly up into the loft. It was late and he was tired. So many messages tonight. Replies too, to be passed back to the fat landlord's ear. He had remembered them all faithfully, and as he fell asleep on his bed of rags, he smiled.

Chapter Three

Da Tinkie's Secrets

Summer grass, wet with misty dew had damped the legs of Magnus' breeks as he walked up through the parks to the croft at Turmtillen, perched precariously on the slopes of Crugness. It was here that he had been born in the lamplight, in the clammy stink of the yellow paraffin glow.

He swore that he would never forget the expression of recognition that passed across his mother's face when she saw him come walking up towards the house. Disbelief, then joy, and her brittle old bones carried her down to meet him, her one good eye gleaming, tear filled, the other sad, half covered by wrinkled skin.

"Magnus . . . ? It canna be . . . It is dee, isn' it?"

"Ja, midder, it's me . . ."

He took hold of her. He felt the warmth of her. The ten years of his wanderings had worn away much of her fitness. She was bent low now, wizened away as old people become. Yet there was something unmistakably alive about Meenie Doull, that went beyond the cares of health. Their embrace lasted minutes, silent.

They walked back to the crofthouse, still clinging to each other, as if uncertain whether the moment was real, and so unwilling to let go the manifestation of it.

Magnus entered the world of his youth, stooping low to cross the threshold, and found himself a giant in the place of his memory. He had allowed himself to expand the dimensions of the tiny house, recalling perhaps the view he had of it when he was a boy. His vision had become time-becalmed.

She made him sit down by the fire. He started to tell her all that he had done and seen, but her first concern was to feed him. She gave him freshly baked bannocks, kirn milk, and butter, the best she had in the house. He began to talk again, but she cut him short, fixing him with her one-eyed stare.

"Magnus," she said, "Whar du's been, and whit du's done, I'm no cairn aboot. Du's here noo."

He laughed, but in his heart he felt a burning need to talk. He wanted to tell her that he had never forgotten about her; that she'd always been in his mind, although he hadn't been in touch. He wanted to tell her the endless churning of his mind that had brought him to the point where he knew that unless he returned to Mirkwick, he could have no future. The past would have absorbed him so totally that regret would have stifled his free spirit. He knew now that all the brawls and the binges and the brothels had been an escape. He had tried to draw a veil across the past, to hide it from himself; had tried to shut off everything that made him who he was. Impossible. There were too many memories, too many chinks in his armour.

He had sacrificed his youth in a vain attempt to forget his boyhood. Oh the waste! He realised it all now. Sometimes he thought he must have known it all along. Images floated into his mind at the strangest of times in the strangest of places. Once, in a whore's bed in Naples he had suddenly seen his father, as clear as a frosty sky, in the corner of the room, angrily chastising him and his way of life. The shock this ghost gave him put an end to his night of pleasure, but when thinking it all out later, he realised that it was his own guilt that had given rise to the ghost.

And now he was resolved to try to right the past. If

not to clear himself of suspicion, then at least to live down the dramas of his past life. It would not be easy, yet unless he did so, he knew he could have no future. Not in Mirkwick, nor elsewhere. For he was a prisoner of his conscience. He had done the cowardly thing when faced with difficulty. He had taken Haakie Manson's advice, and not stopped running for ten long wearisome years. He left his mother to face the tongues of the parish alone, to run the croft. He had deserted her.

For most women, this task would have been impossible. The work alone would have broken their spirit. Not Meenie Doull. She eked out an impoverished existence from the croft at Turmtillen, working like a beast of burden, and she supplemented her income as she had always done. For Meenie Doull was the possessor of the secret knowledge of healing. She prepared lotions and emetics from the recipes given to her by her mother, and it was to her that the people of Mirkwick came when illness struck one of them down. Reluctant they were, for Meenie had been cast out from village society after the affair of the murder. But they came all the same and paid her prices.

And at nights when the work was done, and her bones ached, she would take out the cards that the tinkie had given her, and lay their mystic faces out on the lace tablecloth, in the sacred shape of the cross. The future in a symbolic code was revealed to her. Aald Meenie had the sight.

She recalled the night the tinkie had appeared. Out of nowhere, he stood at her door, a tall curly-haired man, with deep brown eyes, impenetrable.

He spoke English, but with an accent Meenie had never heard the like of. He told her of his sick child, and that he believed she had the powers of healing.

"Maybe," she replied, cautiously.

The man described the ailment, a fever, he said. The child mumbled in a strange language, sometimes broke out and screamed as if enduring a terrible nightmare. Meenie listened carefully. She asked if the child had said ought they could understand.

The tinkie lowered his eyes.

"She spoke of a sea serpent, wriggling around her, entwining itself with her."

Together they set out for the tinkie camp at Lettagill, beyond the hill dykes of Mirkwick. Meenie administered an emetic to the girl that night, in the yellow light of the tinkie's fire. The sick girl vomited violently, and afterwards they immersed her in the cold water of the burn of Lettagill. The shock brought her out of her comatose state.

"Look amongst your own for the cause," Meenie whispered to the tinkie. "The serpent she saw was a man, and that man has interfered with her."

This seemed to make some sense to the tink. He screwed his eyes up, and fixed them on a lad who had watched the careful ceremony of healing with agitated gaze.

"I believe I know the one you speak of," he said, "but now I must pay you for your skills."

He took her to a low tent made of thick canvas stretched over a whalebone frame. It was then that he gave her the cards.

"I have no pieces of siller to reward you with, but I have an ancient knowledge which might, if used correctly, benefit you far more. For I believe that you have the sight, and that you will understand what I have to tell you."

It was early morning before Meenie left the tinkie camp. The mysterious words of the man had drawn out the significance of the cards, and she left with a new and bursting knowledge. He had described in detail their symbolism, had talked in fine words of the Major and Minor Arcana. He had given her the knowledge she required to use the cards.

They rested in her small knapsack, light on her back, a valuable acquisition, as she strode out over the hills back to Turmtillen. The gentle dawn light was drying the mildew from the enshadowed valley of Lettagill. Tired she was, but refreshed in her new learning.

It took time for her to come to feel the cards to be part of her. To understand their patterns instinctively, without having to refer to the tuition of the tinkie. But years passed, and Meenie mastered them with her instincts her tool. She never saw the tink again. He and his camp slipped away into the mists as mysteriously as they had come, and only Meenie had seen them. It was this fact that made her come to believe that their presence at Mirkwork might not have been altogether earthly. Who could say? Trows might have given rise to the tinkie camp, but it made no difference. She had the cards.

They were beautiful. Brightly coloured, and lettered in a language Meenie could not understand. She would spread the Tarot out on the table by the window, silently slipping into a trance-like state, where her conscious mind subsided, and she became the instrument of the future. The haze of the present cleared. In her mind's eye, a vision formed, pieced together by the seemingly random order of the cards. She had seen Magnus more than once whilst he had been at the sailing, and she had followed his travels closely. Not through the maps of the world, but the travels of his spirit from boy to man. She had watched the evolution of his soul, and it was this that caused her to be so little surprised by his return to Mirkwick.

She had known for years that the day would come when he would stand in the lea of the house of Turmtillen and look on the croft as his home. But she also knew that this day could not come until Magnus himself was ready for it.

All that Magnus so dearly wished to explain to her, she already knew. All through the ten years of his exile, she had watched him through the cards, and knew what was in his heart.

"Mair tae?" she asked.

Magnus nodded, mouth full of bannocks and cheese.

"Midder," he began again. "I warrant I owe dee . . ."

"Magnus," she soothed, placing her bony old hand among his wiry hair, "I ken whit du's endured, an I ken why du's come back."

The benign expression of tenderness on her face calmed him.

"Ja," he said, "Du likely does."

"Du'll want ta ken all 'at's happened here," she said.

"Aboot Nina, maybe."

Magnus looked at her oddly. What had happened to Nina?

"I suppose she's married noo, midder. Is dat whit du his to tell me, for if it is, and du's faerd I'll tak' it ill, du needna be. Lord kens I couldna expect her to wait for me. I couldna promise I'd be back."

Meenie said nothing. She always liked Nina. Before the business with Tammas Pole, she and Magnus were set to marry. When he ran from the law, she was, unknown to him, with child — his. Her folk, when they saw the all too prominent bulge, disowned her. A murderer's slut. Meenie offered her a home at Turmtillen, but she refused. She said it would be too near to the memory. The child was still-born and Nina's heart properly broken if it wasn't before.

"Na, she no' married . . . ," Meenie breathed.

Magnus looked at her in surprise.

"No? Dan whar is she?"

"Magnus, she's had a hard time o' it. She was carryin' dy bairn."

He leapt up from his chair, knocking over his tea cup.

"My bairn. Whar is she, Midder?"

His mother retreated to the tiny window. She looked out over Mirkwick lying below on the flat sandy plain, out to the pier, and the Haa House, the shop and the Böd; the factor's house and the smithy, and there, by the shore, the old stone building, where Nina lay waiting for her callers. Her flowering passed, self-indulgent grief her spur.

"Magnus, she's a hoor. She keeps open shop for da ships dat anchor here."

In confusion and disbelief, his mind refused to accept the information.

"Du's lyin'."

"Why would I lie aboot it, boy? Does du think I want to hurt dee? But it's better du hears it fae me, dan some gossip's mouth. Lord kens, dere's plenty dat'll take pleasure in telling dee."

He slipped back into the chair, shock-eyed.

"It's no' her fault, Magnus. It never has been. She's just floated along in da tide laek so many, never strong enough to swim against it. She was just a ting o' lass when du left, carryin a murderer's bairn, for dat's whit dey call dee here. Her family turned against her, she had nobody to help her. I tried, but she'd take nothing fae me. Her grief and her shame were heartfelt, Magnus, believe me. It's come atween her and her reason."

Magnus said nothing. Meenie's heart went out to him. Yes, he was thirty, but he was just a boy inside. A boy that believed he could come back to Mirkwick and right all the wrongs with a few chosen words. But Time doesn't stand still. The longer the tears in the tapestry are left, the wider they become, till there is no mending them.

All the same, she dearly wished that someone else could have been the one to break his illusions.

"And the bairn?" he asked.

"It was still-born, Magnus. It never even saw da light o' day."

Tears formed in the corners of his eyes. His vision blurred. He threw his head onto the table in front of him. A sob so sorrowful that he was unable to repress it broke from his lips.

Peerie soul, formed perfect in the womb, no breath will pass thy lips. Thy life is carried in the belly of thy mother, ends when she presses thee from her side. Sorrow of the still-born, gone to dust and decay ageless, without a regret or a worry. Small features, thumb-nail size, fated never to grow.

Nina lay in the drowsy slumber following the birth. Her hair was knotted in sweat, tears of pain and ecstasy dried to her cheeks. She did not know. The skin of her stomach wrinkled soft and empty now, her burden gone. The smell, the wonderful inimitable smell of new life pervaded her senses as she slept. When she awoke, the smell of death mingled in. The horror of the loss dumbfounded her. In its tiny hands, the life line was erased, the stalk broken.

Months passed in the grip of the burning liquor. Her head pounded with the pain of loss. Magnus gone and now her child, the part of him that he had left to her, dead. She drank feverishly, in the tiny room above the store Haakie Manson had provided for her, on certain conditions. He sent her a boy from the ship swaying in the wick one October day when the eyes of the parish were fixed on their hearths. She gave him solace in her bed.

He left her early, when the storm had quietened. She awoke to find him gone, his blonde Scandinavian boy's face a single night in her memory. His ship now far away and the only trace of that night that remained was his money, tucked under her pillow.

He was the first. She was hungry no more. Haakie looked after her. She cured her caller of his homesickness and he eased the ache in her stomach. It was easy then. It was what was left to her, this love for sale business. She cared nothing for the tongues that scarred her reputation. She had no ego left to protect.

It was all that was left to her. Memories and money tucked under the pillow.

Chapter Four

The Word Spreads

The wind swept across Mirkwick, forcing the banks of tall summer grasses to point south in sweeps like waves of growth. The gale never slackened. Animals took shelter where they could. The tawny white shapes of the sheep could be seen, curled up, huddled under the ruined walls of abandoned crofts. Homesteads that had once housed families, now a mere rumble of moss-beset stones. Floors that had been kissed by straw brooms daily were now carpeted in sheeps pirls, dotted and squelched under prodding hooves. The sheep had taken over. Lairds had chased human life to the colonies in order to make the estate more profitable. Nature quickly reclaims from Man. A few years ago, children skirled and played and men smoked pipes by firesides, settled in the resting chair. Those same children were now growing in very different places, learning a new way to live.

And the wind of rumour and assumption whistled about Mirkwick too, that day, echoing, howling in the mouths of the people.

"Magnus Doull's back!"

Within a day, all but those on the outlying crofts were aware of his presence in the parish. No one knew why he had come back, but all agreed no good would come of it.

The debate surrounding Tammas Pole's death began afresh. Some were certain that Doull was guilty, and others remembered that Tammas had many enemies. But few had time for Magnus. It wasn't just the murder. He'd been a loud-mouthed, cocky fellow, and had offended many people by telling them the truths they preferred not to hear.

They talked. Of course they talked. Wasn't that normal? But it was a long time ago, the murder. The past was better left as it was. Raking it up, uncovering graves of ill-will and misfortune, what good could come of it? Bones and stench, decay and ruin. That would be the only thing they'd find.

That was one thought. It was probably the majority view; but the few felt far more strongly than the many.

Isabella Agnes was in the kitchen at the manse, boiling a piece of mutton for the minister's dinner, when Creepin' Ertie delivered the note to the Reverend Cunningham.

She dried her hands on her apron and went to see who it was. She watched through the cracked-open door, as the letter exchanged hands. She heard voices mutter.

Steam clouded the air of the kitchen as she cooked. Curiosity like clouds fed Isabella's thoughts. What would Ertie be doing delivering letters to the minister, especially on a night like this?

After the dinner was over, the minister, patting his stomach and blessing Isabella's cooking, retired to his study. Isabella cleared the table. She saw the opened letter lying there by his pudding plate. Temptation needled her, pointing with invisible fingers to a secret.

She took the dishes through to the kitchen and put the bachelor's plates into the sink. Hot water from the brass kettle poured into the basin made clouds of steam again. Her resolve fogged as inquisitiveness niggled her.

She went back to the diningroom with the pretence of stoking the fire. The letter was still there. The minister still in his study. She put a peat on the fire, bit at a ragged fingernail, and crossed to the table. She picked the letter up, and turned her back to the study door.

She took the single sheet of paper from the envelope. It was from Haakie Manson. Her eyes flitted quickly over the note . . . The creak of a door. The study door! Adrenalin rushing for fear of being caught snooping, she collected her senses, grabbed the letter, stuffed it into the envelope, smoothed it out, and cast it back onto the table just as she heard the minister's monotone voice.

"Ah here you are Isabella, I was just looking for the letter. Did you ah . . . see it anywhere perchance?" He had a peculiar habit of hesitating in mid sentence when ill at ease.

"I . . . ah . . it's . . ."

Isabella flustered, gestured to the table. The minister looked at her closely.

"Are you . . . ah feeling all right? You look very peaky?"

Red-faced, she ran from the room. She took her coat from the cupboard under the stairs, and, flapping like a mother bird whose nest is threatened she fluttered out to the front porch.

Once out of shelter of the manse, the pressure of the North wind on her slim figure forced her to stoop forward. Her head filled up with desperate detached thoughts, scrambling for attention in her head.

So he was back! Hate intensified. She trembled. The past flooded back, reborn, phoenix-like.

O Tammas Tammas, dear young husband that he'd been. She pictured his boyish face, but saw it blotted by the red hair of Magnus Doull. That devil who had led her good man away to the depths of drunken debauchery only months after their wedding, and then had killed him.

In the faint crimson days of Hairst, he had left her,

for the comfort of the bottle. In a faint crimson evening, he had died, his head crushed by an awesome blow. His poor child's face screwed up into a horrible expression of pain and fear.

And now Magnus Doull was back in Mirkwick. Evil man, son of a witch, and maybe a witch himself, the way he had called up the de'il's legions to spirit him away from the gallows. But Isabella Agnes would face them. She and her God. He would be her strength and comfort in the battle, till this time justice was done, and Magnus Doull hanged!

Isabella Agnes climbed the steps to her one roomed home. She looked sadly at the neighbouring house, where Nina the comforter lived. That whore would be happy now that he was back, thought Isabella bitterly!

An ache of hatred burned in her soul, but the shock was passing. Sadness like the wailing of a lamenting fiddle far off damped the flame inside her. She began to cry. Tears found their way through ready formed routes in the wrinkles of her face, young, yet so old. Her prematurely white hair, dishevelled by the wind fell into her face, and became lank and wet in the force of her anguish. She wept horrible wretching sobs, springing up from the depth of her.

The tap and shuffle step of Creepin' Ertie crossed the cobbles outside. Isabella Agnes, hysterical, did not hear him, but he heard her, his ears cocked as ever to the sounds in Mirkwick.

The uneven stride stopped for a minute. The rumble and whoosh of a wave unfolding on the pebbly beach absorbed the sobs. Creepin' Ertie walked on. Maybe it was the sound of the storm he had heard. A bird, perhaps, lost in the gale, or maybe it was one of the Selkie women Seemon had told him about, crying for a lost love.

He let his fancy run away with him, as he trudged through the dark night, back to his bed at the smithy.

Nina woke with the sound of her lover rising to catch the tide. She lay motionless in the bed as he dressed, cursing his braces, which tangled about his legs.

When the door slammed shut and the footsteps clattered down the stairs into the dawn light, she arose. She took the greasy banknote and crossed to the stove, which she raked, and boiled a kettle.

She washed in the cold morning air, shaking the sluggishness from her mind. She pulled faces in the mirror, sticking her tongue out to examine it.

Haakie Manson's message lay heavy in her mind. She made a pot of tea, and sat down to wait for the hours to pass, until she could go to see him. A woman in her position had to wait. Tongues would have wagged had she visited Haakie early in the morning, just as certain as had she paid him a call at night.

"Something that would interest her greatly."

What could it be?

She traced the time through the movements of the sun across the heavens. All night long the gale had continued, but now it was dying away.

Sounds of the morning at the small harbour below: boats setting out to sea, men calling, muttering, smoking, sorting lines and tackle. Youthful voices questioning, aged mumbles replying, scolding impudence, explaining. The cackle of the maas. The stinging clang of the hammer on the anvil. Lapping, hushing sea at the pierside and beach. A dog far off barking, women going to the pump for water.

Nina lay on her bed, sipping her tea. She listened to the voices at the pump, one of the favourite places for the exchange of news.

They often talked about her.

"Anidder foreigner in her bed. Norske."

"Shameless . . ."

They often talked about her. Nina took it all with a wry smile. She had heard it all before.

"The Lord'll see her sins are punished . . ."

Sometimes, when their comments reached the limits of credibility, Nina would open her window and shout down to them. This made the affair all the more sport for them. It was a kind of game they played, the women pulling water from the well, and the sailor's slut, reclining after her work was over.

Nina listened.

She heard the shrill voice of the shopkeeper's wife, talking to someone from the Haa, a servant girl no doubt.

The squeak of the pump masked the secret, but Nina heard enough.

"Noo he's back, he'll git whit he should have had ten years ago. They hang murderers, you ken."

It could be none other.

She leapt from the bed and ran to the window. But the women had gone, carrying their buckets of water.

Nina felt her heart thump. She shivered. The photograph! The one he had sent her from Liverpool, with the ill-trained words scrawled on the back!

"I *will* see you again, my love. Magnus."

She was scared to look at it, but something forced her to. What fire burned in his eyes! And now he was back, as he had promised.

A confusion of emotions twisted in her breast. What was it she felt, she asked herself? Love? Or Shame? Or Anger?

What would he think of the way she lived? The awful truth of her painted appearance stared at her from her mirror. For the first time, she saw what she was. A whore.

Not one secret of womanhood left to her. The rouge, the dirty money! She felt sick. She wanted to vomit, but she couldn't. She wanted to cry but she couldn't. All emotions had been stifled long ago, so long ago that she had forgotten them. She knew only suppression and cynicism. How many times had she laughed spitefully at that message of hope inscribed on the back of that photograph? How long was it since she had ceased to believe in it? That was why Haakie Manson wanted to see her!

She began to dress hurriedly. She couldn't find anything. One shoe of a pair, nothing fitted. Her world, balanced so precariously on the weak foundation of self-indulgent pity, crumbled slowly about her. She *did* care about something. She cared about him. It was all wrong.

Robert Williamson felt the lock snap open on the heavy shop door. Eight-thirty as usual.

He stopped on the doorstep, and looked about him, as if recording a vision of nature to sooth him while he poured over accounts and ledgers, alienated from the outside.

Waves still crashed against the rocks at Crugness, propelled by a forceful swell out at sea, legacy of the storm. The shopkeeper picked out a figure, collecting driftwood from the freshly mown tang that the gale had ripped from the seabed. It was Aald Seemon.

The roar of the furnace nearby echoed between the buildings of the pierhead. Robert Williamson thought of Creepin' Ertie, sweeping floors in the smithy, and of the message the cripple had brought from Haakie Manson the night before. Maguns Doull had returned to Mirkwick, on the very same steamer as the merchant and his wife. Strange that he had not recognised the red hair.

Of course, something would have to be done. They couldn't allow him to live among them, untried and unchallenged. The man was accused of being a murderer. He would have to answer the charges laid at his door.

He entered his place of business. Familiar smells

greeted him — soap, tobacco, salted fish. And a host of others, mingled together to form a distinctive melange.

He went behind the counter, lifting the wooden gate. In his small office stood his desk, home of the great leather bound ledger he kept all his affairs in order with. All entries must be in the neatest handwriting. Young Peter Jacobsen had shown particular aptitude in this direction. In all directions, come to think of it.

Robert was pleased with the progress his young assistant had made. He was punctual, polite, and clever too. In time, perhaps, the business would fall to him. Robert had no son to inherit, and Peter had some interest in his daughter Agnes, which might develop. Robert would encourage it. Of course his wife would oppose the match, but then she tended to forget that her own background was a poor croft. And they had married successfully. Robert Williamson preferred to think of Agnes married to a man capable of hard and honest toil, than say, someone with a bit of a name, but no character.

At that moment Peter Jacobsen arrived.

"Wind's fallen awa'," he observed.

The shopkeeper grunted. He breathed heavily through his nose, with a kind of snort, causing his moustache to twitch. He pushed the door of his office and it squeaked shut. He must think. He needed to find a plan to sort out this murder business. People expected it of him. He held a position of no little importance in the community, and was one of those who felt responsible for the smaller acts of government neglected by the less public-spirited.

Besides, his wife expected it, and that was a spur indeed. First, he would have to organise a meeting. He would need all the people of substance: the factor, the minister and perhaps someone from the Haa, though the chances of them attending were slim; the kirk elders, and of course, Haakie.

He took a piece of paper, jotting the names down,

sucking his moustache. The bell on the shop door tinkled. He heard a murmur of voices, and stooped so he could see through the crack in the wood pannelled walls of the office. It was the widow Johnson with her eggs to sell, poor woman. She had no time for mourning her dead husband. Too many mouths to feed.

Robert Williamson went back to his list of names. When the woman left the shop, he called out to Peter.

"When you get a spare moment, there's something I'd like you to do for me."

The assistant entered the office.

"I'd like you to copy out a letter, inviting these folk to my house on Monday night. Something like . . . ah . . . 'to discuss the urgent question of Magnus Doull's return . . .' You'll know what to write . . .?"

Peter glanced over the list of names.

"Magnus Doull? Wha's he, Mr W?"

"Never you mind. You'll hear soon enough, no doubt. But I'll just say that he was someone we hoped would never be back. It's ten years since he left. You'd have been seven. I dare say that your folk wouldn't have told you about it. But it was a scandal indeed, a true mystery . . ."

He grunted again, through his nose. He turned again to his desk, and started flicking through pages of the ledger. It was the signal for Peter to leave.

Truth to tell, Robert Williamson did very little for his good living. Peter worked hard, from dawn to dusk, while the old merchant sat smoking and grunting in his office, doing the odd bit of work here and there for appearance sake. He was a decision maker, so he thought, a supervisor, watching over things. Peter and his helpers ran the business, but Robert was the brain behind it all. Or so he imagined.

Suddenly, heels clicked on cobbles up the narrow alley between the rear of the shop and the alehouse. Robert squinted out the window to see who it was, and caught sight of Nina hurrying by, towards Haakie Manson's back door.

He recalled how close she and Magnus had been before the incident, and nodded knowingly. Why, hadn't it been his bairn that she was carrying when her folk threw her out? So Haakie had been in touch with her as well. He had no taste when it came to his choice of confidante.

"Dear Lord, protect me from all evil, give me da strength and courage that I might overcome da devil dat taunts me . . ."

Fevered with white passioned pallor, poor Isabella Agnes knelt beside the tiny bed in her one-roomed cell, her knees knuckle-white on the bare floorboards. She was praying for a vision, a form of guidance that could help her trap the man she hated.

"Take my soul, O God, deliver me into Thy will, that I may become da instrument of Thy Good."

In deep prayer, mystic bond, she tensed and slipped through the levels of the spirit, hoping for divine inspiration.

"Guide me, O Lord, show me the way to do Thy Will."

Her eyes tightly sealed from sight, in tabernacle void, she waited for the sign. Minutes passed, hours, it seemed, and still no realisation. What could be the matter? Had she not emptied herself of all selfish thoughts? Ah, but the Lord moves in mysterious ways! He would show her when she was ready, when she least expected, and then Isabella Agnes would know what part she must play in the tapestry of tears unfolding over Mirkwick.

Oblivious to all outside sounds bar the absorbent hush of the sea, she failed to hear even the uneven stride of Creepin' Ertie climb the steps to her door.

The tap of his hand on the door startled her.

"Who is it?"

"Arturo. I must see you, Isabella."

She went to the door and opened it a fraction, suspiciously.

"Whit do you want?"

"It is important, Isabella, I must see you."

She let the door swing open fully and stood back to let the cripple enter. He cast his eyes to her feet, uneasy.

"I . . . know something, Isabella, that troubles me greatly. It is a burden I can hardly bear. For I feel that I ought to tell this secret I was entrusted with . . ."

She glowed at his sincerity.

"I ken, Arturo, what your secret is. You need not break your confidence. I suppose dat everybody kens noo, dat Magnus Doull is back at Turmtillen."

His face warmed, his burden lifted.

"I felt that I should tell you. I could not decide whether I should keep the secret I was entrusted with, or whether I should be forced to tell you because of my respect."

She bade him sit on the only chair in the room.

"I have been praying, Arturo, I have asked the Lord for his guidance, in order dat I do the right thing . . ."

The cripple smiled, confidante of the true faith.

"And has he answered your prayers?"

"No, alas, not yet, but He will, when He is ready. I must wait, I must believe, and He will show me when I have proved my faith. I canna describe it, but inside, I ken He will."

"It is a wonderful faith which allows you this knowledge. Your are a truly religious woman, Isabella. A true Christian."

She blushed at this welcome flattery.

"I try, Arturo, to do what I ken is right. I may tell you I have some evil thoughts, thoughts of violent revenge, but da Lord has comforted me."

"Pah, who wouldn't feel vengeful in your position, Isabella."

"I loved him so much, Arturo, my Tammas. He was a good man, despite what they said about him."

"Of course, he was kind to me."

She went to the press and opened it.

"You must go now. We don't want tongues wagging. Tell me, have you any bread?"

He shook his head, like a schoolboy aware of an impending gift.

"Then take this brönie, with my blessing for your thoughtfulness."

She wrapped the bannock in a cloth and handed it to him.

"And may the Lord bless you, kind lady," he answered.

She smiled with self-righteous smugness.

"He will, in time."

Arturo turned again to thank her, and she put her finger to her lips. Instead of speaking, he lifted her smooth worn hand like a washer-woman's, and kissed it repeatedly. She drew it away from him, unsettled, and closed the door.

Arturo, bread in cloth under arm, became the wretched Creepin' Ertie again. Only in this small dwelling was he called by his christened name. He was especially honourable there, because of this.

It reminded him of his boyhood days spent in the dusty backstreets of Padua. It reminded him of the sweet melodic language he had once spoken, and had now all but forgotten. Italy. How he missed it! How he wished he could return! But what would his family want with a crippled son, assuming they were still alive? It was just a dream. These cold northern shores were his home now, and he would never leave Mirkwick. He was part of it now.

A tear appeared in the cripple's eye. He broke off a piece of the bread and began to chew on it. He had not eaten since the previous day, and although this was not unusual for him, he had done so much walking in the course of his errands for Haakie Manson that he was ravenous.

All that work, and not a penny in his pocket. Still, Haakie would repay him in time. He always did, eventually, in one way or another.

Dusk was falling over Mirkwick. The pierhead was deserted. Ertie began to walk towards the smithy. In the half-dark, behind the shop store, he heard a voice hushing. He looked. Two figures disappeared into the shadows. It was Peter Jacobsen and Agnes of the shop.

Ertie carried on, pretending he hadn't seen them. Young love should be left in peace, he thought.

A light in the Haa house caught his eye. He had never been inside that huge house, not in all the years he had spent in Mirkwick, though he had once been taken into the servant's quarters by one of the maids who had taken a liking to him. She gave him beef from the larder. He had never tasted the like; so rich.

He supposed that there were all kinds of devils lurking inside those walls. Ghosts of dead men, unhappy in their wealth, destroyed by the evil greed. Arturo, poor and crippled, had no wish for riches. In his poverty, he had so much more — his pride and self respect.

So many people trusted him. Why, only tonight the factor had given him a letter for Robert Williamson, and he had delivered it without so much as a glance at it. How many others would have resisted such a temptation? Not many, but, he, Arturo, had. Hadn't he?

And on he went, shuffling along, muttering to himself, dragging his disfigurement proudly behind him.

Robert Williamson surveyed the letter once again. Its cold tone angered him.

Dear Mr Williamson,

My thanks for bringing to my attention the return of the popularly accused murderer, Magnus Doull. I regret that I am unable to attend your meeting on Monday first, but I shall give the matter some thought as you suggest,

Yours,
T. Sutherland.
Factor for the Estate of Mirkwick.

The handwriting stared at him, cold and aloof. There was no clue to the factor's feelings on the matter. It seemed as if he was treating the whole affair lightly. Williamson scowled. Well, he'd go ahead with his plan regardless. It wasn't unusual, after all, for him to be left to do the needful, without the help of those whose jobs it was by rights.

D

Chapter Five

Good Parishioners

Good parishioners. That was how the minister classified those of his flock that gathered in the house next to the shop that night, to debate what they should do about the scandal of Magnus Doull's return.

"That he should have the bladder to show his face," cried Mrs Williamson, horror-struck.

"Gall, dear, the expression is 'have the gall', her husband corrected.

"Well, gall, bladder, it's all the same, isn't it? Maybe you have a commanding knowledge of anatomy, dear, but the rest of us haven't. But we do know the difference between right and wrong, and we won't have that murderer in our midst."

Mrs Williamson had a large mouth. Her husband's main complaint regarding her was the perpetual ringing of her voice in his ears.

"You can't call him a murderer, I'm afraid. There was no real evidence against him, remember, and nothing can be proved," the minister pointed out.

"And didn't he just prove himself guilty by up and running away like that?" interjected Mr Williamson.

This was the strongest possible evidence in the minds of the community against Doull.

"And mind you, he never denied it at the time," Mrs Williamson reminded, passing out a tray of home-bakes among the assembled company.

The good parishioners: Mr and Mrs Robert Williamson, hosts. The Reverend Cunningham. The kirk elders, with their wives: Bob and Tamar o' da Links, Peter Jacobsen and Margaret from Farpund, the parents of Robert's assistant. Albert and Mary o' Abberty, and lastly, Aald Seemon with his wife Bessie, the midwife and nurse. His dear wife, as he referred to her.

And of course, Haakie, though he was in attendance, not for his kirk connections, but for his position in the community.

"Da question is," said Seemon, "not whether he's guilty or not, but what we're going to do to find out da truth."

They all nodded in agreement. Seemon could always be relied upon to keep objectives in mind. Although he was past seventy now, and no longer went to the fishing, he had, in his day, been the best Haaf skipper in the area. His knowledge of the coastline and the fishing grounds were second to none.

He lit his pipe, stuffing it full of shag tobacco. His wife whispered something in his ear, and he glanced at Mrs Williamson who was eyeing him with displeasure.

"Not in here, if you don't mind," she advised.

Seemon thought to himself what a dreadful life Robert o' da shop must have, with that creature at his throat all the time, but he obligingly extinguished the smoke. Truth to tell, he didn't really want to get involved in all this, but being a kirk elder, he felt it his duty. In his opinion, the assembled crowd could be a dangerous bunch when fired up with their self-righteousness, bar himself and Haakie Manson.

And he'd never been all that sure of the truth of that night ten years ago, when Tammas Pole had gone to meet his Maker. At the time, there was a lot of subterfuge and cunning in the air. Tammas had made himself a few enemies in those months before his death. No, Seemon never made a snap judgement, unlike Haakie, his best friend besides his boat. They were very different characters indeed, but somehow seemed to complete each other with the mix of snap decision and long deliberation.

Their friendship had been compounded through the hours that they had spent in the Böd, Seemon lingering over his pints of ale, discussing the topics of the day with Haakie.

"But dere can be no certainty in this matter," Seemon continued. "None can call another a murderer lest he has proof, for such an accusation is an offence under another law, libel, or some such thing."

The minister confirmed this.

Seemon began to light his pipe again, forgetful of his hostesses wishes, and he was admonished by Bessie, his kindly wife. She was a good soul, Bessie.

"A finer wife, I could never have found," Seemon would say, a little tipsy, the rum warm in his throat, and Bessie would blush like a teenager.

"Ging awa', du aald föl . . . "

Seemon was right as usual. They couldn't accuse Magnus Doull of anything. But as Margaret Jacobsen said, "I'll make sure he canna spread his evil influence on my bairns, in God's name I will do it."

To this fiery statement of religious zeal, they drank a toast of sweet sherry provided by Haakie Manson. It seemed to loosen everyone's collars, not least of them, Mrs Jacobsen's, who, surprised and pleased by the reception her outburst had received, went on to talk still more loudly.

"I believe there is nothing more important in a child than purity, and dat dis should be the parent's aim, over and above even education."

This took everyone by surprise. It seemed she had discovered an eloquence hitherto unknown within her. In fact, she had read this in a small textbook on the Christian approach to parenthood given to her by the Reverend Cunningham's predecessor.

It was surprising how widespread was this view among the respectable houses of the area, judging by the reaction this statement aroused. Everybody agreed, and Bob o' da Links even repeated the whole sentence to his wife, who was a little deaf. She clasped her hands when he had done so, and the heads nodded once again.

Mrs Jacobsen decided not to miss the opportunity to impress, and raised her voice again.

"In fact, my midder used to say dat a clean soul was more important dan a clean shift," she trilled.

She giggled at this, it being an old family joke, but the others were taken aback. Peter Jacobsen lent across and whispered something in his wife's ear, expressionless like an undertaker.

Her giggling stopped immediately, and she turned a bright scarlet. The ensuing silence Mrs Williamson let develop just far enough to thoroughly embarass Margaret Jacobsen without entirely humiliating her.

"More tea before you go?" she hinted.

"No thank you," blushed Margaret, "I . . ," but her comment was arrested by the firm hand of her husband gripping her arm.

They left promptly, making the excuse that they couldn't leave the boys on their own too long. Mrs Williamson saw them out into the night.

"Peace go with you," she said, knowing that would be the last commodity present in Farpund tonight. She had enjoyed Margaret's *faux pas* enormously. Ever since Peter her son, and Agnes had shown an interest in each other, Mrs Jacobsen had seemed to think that gave her the right to treat Mrs Williamson as an equal. Well, of course, there was nothing between them, they were only children.

She was just about to close the door, when a voice called out to her from somewhere along the road, near the Haa House.

She went outside again. A figure came running

through the dusk, with cloak fluttering behind. Mrs Williamson's sharp eyes recognised the girl who had travelled on the steamer from Lerwick with she and her husband.

"Mrs Williamson?" the girl panted, curtseying, which pleased the shopkeeper's wife greatly.

"Yes, my dear?" she answered sweetly.

"The mistress says she is sorry she cannot come to your meeting, but that she will send me in her place, as she is otherwise engaged."

"I see . . . "

She must think we are children, thought Mrs Williamson, to send this child here!

"Well, you'd best come in then," she said, not bothering to disguise her displeasure.

Ellen Mitchell was no more keen to attend this meeting than Mrs Williamson was to have her here, but, she had felt that she must do as her mistress wished. They entered the ben room, Mrs Williamson first.

"It's Miss Mitchell, from the Haa. Lady Morton's sent her because she's otherwise engaged," she said, trying to impart a little of her feelings without seeming harsh on the girl.

They looked at her in surprise. The conversation turned to the girl.

Seemon winked at her, an unspoken reference to the event of a few days ago, when she had inadvertantly displayed her underwear to the crowd at the pierhead.

"So you're to be the ladies companion?" the minister inquired.

"Not to be, minister, the young lady is," the hostess corrected.

"Yes," said Ellen, embarassed.

"And how do you find your new position, Miss Mitchell?" asked Robert Williamson.

"Oh, it's pleasant enough," she smiled, "Though

I've been there too short a time to really pass judgement.''

''A wise lass dan,'' said Seemon, himself given to long deliberation. ''And where is it you're from?''

''Edinburgh,'' the hostess cut in. ''I know for you told me yourself on the steamer, didn't you?''

''Yes, of course.'' The questions were unsettling the girl.

The minister and Robert Williamson came to the conclusion that as Miss Mitchell knew nothing of the business in hand, the minister should be the the one to explain it all to her.

''Well,'' began the Reverend Cunningham, ''It all started when I was but a novice in my vocation. I recall I arrived here in the spring, and the incident took place at harvest time. Am I right?''

Nods and affirmations. They were warming to the thought of one of the minister's monologues. A fine speaker he was, in and out of the pulpit.

''It was mid-August, I remember, and we had been blessed with a fine summer. The crops were good, and the people were content. You could say well prepared for the winter, for you being a newcomer to the parish, you won't know how harsh these can be here. There had been a bit of celebration when the crops were gathered in. Nothing excessive, you'll understand. Merely the expression of some rather high spirits. But, as always, there were those who didn't know when to stop. The man we're concerned with tonight was one of them. Magnus Doull, a wild young fellow of twenty . . ''

''Nineteen,'' corrected Mrs Williamson.

''Nineteen, then. Ah . . . Oh yes, Magnus Doull. Well, he and another young man one Thomas Pole had been holding a high and mighty time, never out of the influence of the demon drink for a fortnight, getting up to mischief of all kinds. Hindering people at their work, that sort of thing.

Then one night they fell out, right here at the pierhead, in full sight of everyone. They began to brawl, and two of the fishermen had to pull them apart. Seemon himself, here, was one of them. Doull was as hot-tempered as one of the devil's own, and he swore that he would kill Pole. We have plenty of witnesses to that. However, they separated, their fun having soured at last, or so we thought. But it seems it was not so, for the next morning, there amongst the boats that rest in front of the Haa was the body of Pole, with his head crushed under a fearful blow.

Well, feelings ran high, understandably, because of the fight that had occurred earlier in the day. Doull was accused by popular opinion of the murder. I think the good people might have lynched him, had it not been for Seemon, myself and some others making them see sense. For we had no real proof. Not that we weren't determined to find some, but justice, as they say, must be seen to be done.

Doull made no attempt to defend himself. He couldn't remember a thing, so he said. A special constable was contacted to investigate the case, but before he arrived here in Mirkwick, Doull had disappeared. We don't know how or where he went. Well, from that day until the steamer arrived in Mirkwick last Tuesday, we had tried to forget the whole sad episode. But now Doull has appeared again, almost ten years later, and we the good parishioners, have assembled here to try to decide on the action we should take. We feel it's our duty."

Ellen Mitchell listened closely to the tale. All the while, she became more and more relaxed. She felt that this special attention given to her was a kind of welcome.

Everyone waited for a comment from the girl.

Finally, she spoke . . .

"It could be that he didn't kill Pole, but that he ran away because he was afraid."

They were all astounded.

"Why, you sound almost as if you were on his side," remarked Mrs Williamson tersely.

"It's not that," said Ellen, "I'm just trying to see the side which isn't immediately obvious. Like the dark side of the moon," she said dreamily.

No one spoke. Aald Seemon thought to himself that she was a clever one.

She was pretty in an unconventional way. Possibly some trace of childhood still remaining in her adult self, he mused, as she sipped the tea given to her. She was not offered sherry.

Finally, the silence was broken.

"Well, I say that we must do something or not. As Seemon says, it's not our task to determine his guilt, but we must decide on a course of action." It took some seconds for the slower brains to switch their attentions from the comments of Ellen Mitchell.

Seemon nodded.

"I suggest we hear if anybody has any ideas. For myself, I think it best if we wait until da factor is available. It's really his affair, law and order."

"Dat's true enough, Seemon, said Haakie. "It's not our business to meddle, you ken."

Robert Williamson protested.

"I invited the factor here tonight, and got a very offhand reply. You ken yourselves that the folk whose responsibility this is are not the quickest to move, if you'll pardon my frankness, Miss Mitchell. And I believe it most certainly is our business, if there's a murderer running about free."

"If he is guilty."

"We can't afford to wait until the factor decides he has time for us."

"What if he murders one of us, or one of our bairns?"

"Come, come. He's not a maniac," laughed Haakie.

"We can't afford to take the risk," hissed Williamson, becoming annoyed.

"I say we contact the police in Lerwick right away."

There was a degree of approval and disapproval for this motion. They decided to take a vote, and the hands were raised, five in favour, five against. They all looked at Ellen who had not raised her hand at all.

"I don't know enough about the way things are done here, but I agree that the proper authorities should deal with it," she said softly.

This began another argument. Robert Williamson pointed out that the police were the 'proper authorities,' while Haakie said that it was the factor's place to decide, and his alone.

Suddenly, the minister jumped up, looking at his watch, chained to the waistcoat.

"Dear, dear, I'm afraid I'll have to go. I have a Bible class in half an hour."

This was the signal for the meeting of the good parishioners to adjourn.

Mrs Williamson glanced at the American clock her father had brought back from the sailing. It was the only item she had brought to this house that she still cared for.

One by one, the meeting dispersed. They thanked Mrs Williamson for her hospitality. She said "Goodnight" to them at the door, and turned to her husband.

"I don't like that girl, Robert."

Chapter Six

The Curse of Gabriel Erasmusson

Da Haa o' Mirkwick stood three storeys high on the rocky promontory which separated Mirkwick from Mareelwick. It was an exposed position, open to the fierce Atlantic sweeps, but the walls were composed of three foot of stone.

What sweat had brought that stone to Mirkwick! What pores had opened in the name of that house! In 1735, the work had begun, with stone quarried in the south end of Shetland. The crofters themselves were employed to do the heavy labouring work, without wages and without choice.

That was the way it was. They either did as the laird wished, or found themselves turned out into the night, homeless.

The work took forty-one years to complete. It was a grand structure, in keeping with the fashion of the time, and to the minds of the poor folk, it served as a constant reminder of the laird's power. Wherever your feet might have been in Mirkwick, the Haa was always to be seen. The sheer size of the house in comparison with their own miserable hovels symbolised in the vast incontrovertible gulf between ruling class and ruled. Although they lived in the same place geographically, their lives were miles apart.

But the untouchability of the Haa was a myth. A strange curse, born out of the intense hatred of one of the tenants had penetrated the three foot thick walls of the great house.

Gabriel Erasmusson was tenant of Farpund at the time of the building of the Haa. He refused to put aside his own labours to assist in the work. The factor brought him before the laird of the time, a Buchanan, and he was asked why he had not answered the order along with the other men of the parish.

Erasmusson said nothing. His heart was full of rebellion. The laird ordered that he be evicted from Farpund, along with his wife and family. Then Gabriel, with his eyes burning white fire, spat at the Buchanan, and laid the violence of his tongue on him.

"As God is my witness, dis house dat has cost me my livelihood will be accursed. It shall not pass through da lineage of a family beyond two generations. It will be da revenge of fate for da wrongs of dis ruling class."

That is how legend has it. No one knows what became of Gabriel Erasmusson, his sickly wife and four small children. Some say he went to America. But his curse lives on in the walls of that house.

And as in other mysterious tales of the supernatural, no one can say what influence the minds of the accursed themselves had on the outcome of the prophesy. But what is certain is, that as Gabriel had predicted, no second generation had yet inherited the Haa of Mirkwick.

Buchanan himself saw his two sons die before him, and the next owner, one James Scott watched his only daughter reach her barren years childless.

The estate had then been bought by the father of the present laird. He was a fair man, old Robert Morton. He treated his tenants well, and sympathised with the poverty of their existence. He founded a tiny school for the education of their children.

But the estate had been bought with inherited

wealth, and Sir Robert did not possess his father's business acumen. He was not, in truth, prepared for a life as a landowner. He was the second son, and had studied philosophy and literature at St Andrews University, and until his elder brother lost his life, Robert had planned a quiet existence alone with books and bookmen. On his brother's death, Robert came into a tidy fortune, and against the advice of friends, had purchased the estate of Mirkwick from the failing James Scott. He paid more than it was really worth, but he had great plans for the place. Few of them came to fruition. A succession of unscrupulous factors milked the estate for their own benefit.

He died a happy, but partially ruined man, and his son Edward inherited little. He had to borrow money from relatives on the mainland to right the financial mess his father had left him, and proceeded to pay off those loans by extracting from the estate the penny next to rebellion. When that was done, and the people felt a slackening of the harness, they fell to calling him a good laird, fair and just.

He was a man of considerable talent was Sir Edward Morton, and not an unfeeling character. He had watched his father make mistake after mistake by placing trust in those who did not deserve it. He had continually employed men from the mainland of Scotland to run his affairs, and they had almost invariably robbed him when they realised how little he knew and cared about business. Edward was determined not to make this mistake.

He went to the brightest young student of the time, Thomas Sutherland, a local man who had been orphaned and brought up by the old teacher under Sir Robert's guidance, and promptly offered him the job as factor. This caused great surprise in the district, but Edward had his reasons. He reckoned that as long as the factor himself felt some responsibility to his tenants, and what better way to ensure that than for him to be one of them; then he would have to be fair and honest.

Admittedly, Sir Edward did not give Sutherland the powers that previous factors had. But after a time, he came to trust his employee, and so the laird himself was left increasingly to his own pleasures.

He was not the student his father had been. His main desires were port wine and servant girls, a mixture that did not meet with the approval of the Reverend Cunningham. A number of young girls had left the Haa house at Mirkwick considerably more plump than they had been when they arrived, with nought but an empty hand and a bland goodbye.

His wife, the Lady Isobelle had long since ceased to care. She lived a life of deep religious searching, wandering through the big house, prayer book in hand. She encountered the saints in the library, in the gardens, as alive as she, enduring their own particular agonies in the martyrdom of her inner self. She was eccentric or visionary, depending on one's viewpoint. But she herself felt that her meetings with the saints were truly the product of a monastic existence of contemplation, and not the crazed imaginings of an inbalanced mind.

She had a sweetness about her that attracted one and all, despite being an introverted person, by and large. She was adored by the servants and never hid her heart from them. People flocked to her, as if desiring to protect this butterfly from predators.

Even Edward, busy with his sexual intrigues, could not resist her child-like nature, and was in the habit of giving her whatever she wished, which wasn't much, really, considering her catholic preoccupation with the soul.

It came as rather a shock to him, then, that morning over breakfast when she announced quite unexpectedly her wish to have a lady companion.

"A young girl," she said. "A good girl, with whom I can discuss matters of the spirit."

Edward resolved to find such a girl, although puzzled by his wife's sudden change of heart. She had always been such a solitary soul.

He contacted a cousin of his in Edinburgh, the headmaster of a private school for the sons of gentlemen. He arranged to interview a number of young ladies with this position in mind.

Ellen Mitchell was the daughter of a respectable lawyer, well educated and a devout Christian. It had seemed that she was set for a life in Edinburgh's finest circles, the wife of some very important young man. She had all the prercquisites. She was intelligent, atractive and well groomed.

It would not be long before the young men began to fall for her. Or so her parents thought. But it was the very virtues that so suited her for life among the upper classes, and so mapped out her future, that prevented it. Her understanding of Christianity and her humanitarian sympathy drew her across the boundaries of normal social life, and so inspired was she by visions of purity that she felt she could never take her place among creatures of the material world.

She wanted to enter a convent. She fixed her sight firmly on her ideal and would not be wavered. Her parents tried to sweeten her away from her wishes, and then hardened their will too. Months past, and the negotiating table was set aside, both sides believing that the other would soften in time.

Neither did, and so it was that a compromise was reached where both her parents and herself agreed to waive all decisions on her future until her eighteenth birthday. Her father, a friend of the schoolteacher cousin of Sir Edward Morton, arranged her interview.

She went to the interview wearing a new dress, nervous of the unknown ahead of her, but glad that at last she was able to do something. She had tired of the game of will she had played with her parents.

The schoolmaster asked her many questions, that Lady Morton had designed herself, in order to divine the true nature of the applicant. Ellen gave all the right replies, not because she contrived to deduce the answers, but because she was the right person. Fate had designed something new for her. The powers had matched her life with Lady Morton's for a time.

Their discussions, on the day when Ellen arrived, were composed mainly of her ladyship questioning and Ellen, in her thoughtful way, replying as honestly as she could. She probed deep into Ellen's faith, and she was surprised to find in one so young such a profound understanding of Christianity.

Sir Edward watched this with fascination. He had always believed his wife to be incapable of caring for another being in the intense way he desired. He thought she was a solitary person, and so had given her so much space to lead her single life in, that he hardly knew her.

As he watched the two women become closer and closer, a kind of perverse jealousy welled up inside him. Before, jealousy was unthinkable, but now he realised that it was he who had failed to give her what she required from a relationship, and he was hurt, his male pride punctured. Yet he could not dislike Ellen. She was so sweet and pure that there were no faults for him to pick up and swell into a poor opinion.

Ellen brought fresh life to the Haa House. She opened symbolic windows and let the wind of change blow through. She upset a routine life which encapsulated the whole household. The servants fell victims to her charms. Even the old bloodhound softened.

Only James, the laird's son, was adversely affected. Ever since he first set eyes on her on board the steamer, he had been besotted with her. This passion was so overpowering that it distracted him from all other sources of enjoyment. His summer seemed destined to be spent inside an illusion of love, yet for him it was painfully real. He imagined romantic undertones in her words to him, and fancied that she secretly returned his love.

Ellen was far older than James. in all except years. Her maturity far outreached his, and consequently could not help looking on him as a child. This made it all the worse for him. The only way he could bear this unrequited love was to retreat into his world of illusion.

As the days passed and Ellen made no firm sign to him of the love he suspected, he began to build in his mind the image of her as a tease. His love turned to distaste, and then to hatred, as powerful as his love had been, but secret, again in the manner of his original desire. He moped around all summer, making an otherwise contented household uneasy. When the time came for him to return to school, only his mother really missed him. For she so doted upon him that she failed to see his true character.

He was not a pleasant young man, James Morton. He was tremendously condescending to all beneath his social position, and the fishermen of the parish whom he sometimes visited with sneers and impertinent questions often remarked they were glad that old Erassmusson's curse had specified that only two generations of any family would rule over the estate of Mirkwirk.

Chapter Seven

Whaals

Magnus did not venture far from Turmtillen those first few weeks. He had a lot of idle money from his adventures at sea, and set about some necessary repairs to be made to the house. Mr Williamson was reluctant to sell him the materials he needed, but when he saw the money in Doull's purse, he relented. He was above all a businessman.

Magnus even bought an expensive penknife that had lain in the shop for years unsold, because of its high price. Williamson hesitated.

"It'll serve you well, Doull," he said, glad of the silver in hand, but none too sure of the morality of the sale. After all, a knife in a murderer's hand?

Feelings had subsided a little since the shock of Magnus' reappearance. Whilst he was shunned by most folk, Seemon and Haakie always had a word for the exile when they met. He had mellowed. He was resolved to live a quiet life, they agreed.

But the longer Magnus stayed in Turmtillen, the more he felt himself irritated by the easy acceptance of poverty by the poor folk. He had seen cultures in his travels and as he re-absorbed the mood of life in Mirkwick, he couldn't help but feel a sense of tyrannic rule. It wasn't open or obvious. But all the while there was an undercurrent flowing of repression and despotism.

Of course, having experienced other ways of life,

Magnus was privileged. Poor folk of Mirkwick knew only life in Mirkwick, and this, he felt, was the problem. Never having conceived of any other kind of life, they just went on, without complaint, putting up with the all too frequent wrongs done to them. The recent Act of Tenure had been a step in the right direction, he admitted, but still no one really tried to develop the potential of the land and the people. Lairds only wanted what they could gather by easy picking. Travel so expands the horizons that Magnus was outcast not merely by the noses of the people, but by the things in his heart.

He had heard talk of Socialism during his travels, and had read a little in his slow awkward manner — Owen, Saint Simon, Fourier. And now the works of Marx and Engels, who had taken the idea and applied it to a scientific basis. He possessed nought but an average intellect. It was rather his sense of right and wrong which spurred him.

But what was the use of this idealism, whilst the poor people carried on just as they'd always done, making the best of the little they had? Toiling to make a pauper's living. It had been a struggle for Magnus, spurred by his better instincts, to understand even the basic message. How could these folk of narrow horizons be expected to see the futility of their labours?

He resigned himself to repairing the croft of Turmtillen and tried to put his questioning aside. Then, when he felt pleased with his work there, he turned his attentions to the boat which had lain for years by the side of the house, under cover, but unused. Much of the timber had to be replaced. It was a long and exhausting task, but it was more than a handyman's diversion for Magnus. For one thing, the boat had been the proud possession of his late father, and for another, he had developed again a taste for the salty breeze and the swell of the sea.

He worked hard at the boat, hoping that he could use

it to catch a supply of piltocks to salt for the long winter months when fresh food was negligible. It helped him to bear the sadness he felt over Nina, for although he couldn't bring himself to go and see her, his mind spent many long hours with her. All the time, he knew that eventually he must visit her. He couldn't live in a place the size of Mirkwick without coming across her at some point, and it was best that they should say what had to be said at the beginning.

Meenie was overjoyed to see him so intent on his labours. He even attended to some of the heavier jobs about the croft that were traditionally women's work, to save her the trouble.

And all the time, he never mentioned Tammas Pole to anyone. He never had done. His memory of the incident was so rum-soaked that he didn't even know himself if he was guilty. At first he felt himself to be terribly wronged, and was deeply upset by the allegations, but once he was clear of the fingers pointing at him, he was able to take an objective view, and had to admit to himself that he could well have killed him. He had the temper for it, that he knew well enough. It took many years for him to realise he had to go back and face the charges for his own peace of mind.

He finished the repairs to the boat at the end of July, much quicker than he expected. She wasn't big, but big enough for one man. He fished around the rocks off Crugness, below Turmtillen, picking up piltocks and mackerel, and the odd haddock. He seemed to posses that quality vital to all successful fishermen: a sense of where the fish were.

As he left the croft one morning early, on his way to the noost, he heard the sound of voices, and on looking towards the harbour, he saw men agitated, pointing out to sea and making ready. He inspected the sea and out beyond Crugness he saw what the commotion was about.

A school of Caain' whales!

He began to run, and raced across the beach to reach the boats just as they were heading out to sea. Magnus joined in the melee without invitation.

Crews were made up of the first men to arrive, and he plunged through the shallows into a boat. Some of the men were still half asleep it seemed, as they struggled to find a rhythm with the oars, but gradually they slipped into smooth combined action.

Other bodies tumbled into boats, sending sprays of seawater chill into the morning air. It was a scattered armada that put to sea.

Magnus screwed his eyes to the whales, spouting and bathing about a quarter of a mile off Crugness.

The boats headed out to the north-east, circling the school. There was a fair swell, and the spray washed sleepy faces as the oars cleft the ocean, propelling wood through water. They came upon the whales, trapping them against the headland. Men shouted, using whatever means they could to make noise. The whales turned towards land. It was impossible to put a number on them, but judging by the bodies twisting and shining slate-blue, it seemed a worthwhile venture.

The school retreated further and further.

The shouts continued.

When it seemed as if nothing could go wrong, one of the men suddenly threw an anxious pointing finger to the shore.

"Look," he cried.

At first no one heard him, but his crewmates. Gradually word passed from boat to boat, until the noise fell away and there was silence.

All eyes were fixed on the harbour, where three boats, carrying latecomers, were preparing to put to sea. It was a rule of these occassions that all shared equally in the kill, and these men in their eagerness to be in at the death were paying little heed to what was happening at sea.

Magnus breathed, "Dey'll turn dem."

They tried to shout to the boats coming out, but it was hopeless. The whales were aware of the new threat, and the forward progress of the hunt halted. For a second, it seemed as if all might be well, but then quite suddenly, as if making a joint decision after debate, the whales began to swim seaward.

The boats between them and the open sea were now in danger. The whales were oblivious to all obstacles in their panic, and the flotilla was in their way.

Men rowed, according to their position, for safety. As the whales sped towards them, Magnus and his mates seemed in imminent danger. They started to row for the centre of the voe to avoid collision.

Magnus, struck by some inspired thought, shouted.

"Bide whar you are!"

The crew gaped at him in confusion, but he was right; the whales veered north themselves, towards Hulterness and the safety of the ocean.

Other boats took chase, but Magnus' companions merely held their breath, stunned, aware of the mistake they had so nearly made.

The hunters returned to the shore in the same disorderly fashion as they had left. Voices grumbled at the foolishness of the few who had prevented the successful completion of the hunt.

All except the crew of Magnus' boat. They knew how close they had come to disaster, and that it was Magnus' instinct that had spared them. Grudgingly, they muttered their thanks.

But he turned his head from their gratitude. It lay heavy on his heart, the role of hero after so often playing the villain.

He left them to their talk, walking the length of the beach to his own craft, and set about preparing his lines. He watched the crowd disperse. He could hear some of their words come drifting through the stillness.

The story was being told already. It would spread fast. He couldn't help feeling a little satisfied. He'd done a good deed today and possibly saved lives.

Then as if intended as a reminder, his eyes happened to rest on the room above the store, and there she was, leaning out of the window, talking to one of the fishermen. No doubt he would tell her the story. No doubt she would close the window and feel all alone in the world.

He would have to see her. There was too much between them. Words that must be spoken.

He put the oars by thoughtfully, and began to wind the hooked line over the side. What would he say to her? How would he begin? He'd loved whores before. How many seamen hadn't? Yet it was a very different matter to return home and find the whore is your childhood sweetheart. He thought of the child they had conceived. It would have been ten years old near enough, had it lived. How Fate could twist the wholesome and make it rotten!

He pulled the line in, winding it up. He had no heart for the fishing today. A few piltocks to salt, that was all he would have to show for his labours, and hadn't he caught scores already?

He fitted the oars back in rowlocks and pulled for the shore. He would not fish today.

Chapter Eight

Late Vigil

A pale white moon is rising over Mirkwick. The village lies asleep. There is a light frost in the air, showing hoary fingers to the night, plying icy patterns over the fields.

Overhead the sky is clear. The moon is a distant eye, watching, casting faint shadows of recognition. Orion with his three point hunter's belt straddles the heavens. The plough furrows the ghostly soil of space. And seven sisters contemplate as they comb their locks among the mirrors of their blue and empty beauty.

In every house, minds deep in silent longing dream their private dreams. Fishwives in little box beds, hair knotted in bunches on pillows, see the glint of salty scales, of whiting and herring still quivering in the morning sunlight. They dream of peerie purses filled with silver.

And the fiddler lies with his tunes playing in perfect tone and tune. Their rhythm the rhythm of his heart, their beat the beat of life in Mirkwick.

Across the plain of Mirkwick, houses huddle into the natural curves seeking shelter. All sleep. Except one. Somewhere by the walled gardens of the Haa House, a single lamp burns, faint and hardly noticeable.

Thomas Sutherland, the factor, sits crouched writing, over his small desk. He is surrounded by books. His face, hawk-nosed yet sensitive, is illuminated by that single light, and his expression betrays an internal confusion.

It is his birthday. Not that he cares much for that. But he is lonely. It is the home of a scholar, a pleasant room, with a fireplace and a window with a view out over the cove and the shingly beach, full of books. He was the finest scholar of his generation, one which had benefitted so from the tiny school the old laird had set up at the Myres. It was now fallen into decay, the roof collapsed, sad evidence of neglect.

But his brief and unfinished education had led to his position as factor. What an honour he had thought it at first! He was young then, and did not really know what the job entailed. Often it was necessary to discipline people he had known and respected for years. Ach power!

He hardened to it. He took too much pride in his abilities not to. And after a time he began to think of himself as the factor, and not just as a child of Mirkwick. The powers he now had were advantageous in many ways. He could have the pick of the women in the parish. Food and hospitality were his right where ever he travelled.

His mind harked back to his visit to the recently widowed Johnson woman up at the Myres.

She was feeding the hens when he arrived. She looked harrowed and drawn, her thin cheeks showing signs of hunger. Children ran bare-bottomed and dirty-faced about her skirts. There was poverty crying out in their eyes to him.

She greeted him pleasantly, and took him to the house, where she gave him tea and bannocks. As he watched her dart about nervously, first pity and then anger overcame him. What could he do?

There was a beauty about her for all her cares. He watched. She was young enough to pass for twenty-five, not thiry-five.

A sudden irrational desire for her overwhelmed him. He reached out, and heard a voice, his own mutter in her ear.

"I could help you if you'd but let me . . ."

Poor woman. She was so distraught by this. No doubt the thought had possibly entered her own mind, to be cast away from her in disgust.

Then the son had appeared, meeting them in the midst of their abortive embrace. She wriggled from his grip.

The boy stared long and hard. Thomas noticed him swell with anger, and then he had rushed forward with his fists beating, shouting, swearing . . .

Thomas held him tight till the anger subsided into tears.

He left then. What else could he do? He should never have touched her in the first place.

Yet he was so lonely for a real woman's touch.

And he had the problem of Magnus Doull to deal with. At first he hoped that the past might be forgotten, but there were those who were bent on raking it up. The minister and Robert Williamson as always, stirring things.

Sutherland would gladly have let things lie buried. His heart was heavy, and he was alone.

What a birthday!

There were other reasons for his depression. Other matters working on his mind. Matters that must be attended to right away before they brought him deeper into trouble.

He shook his tired head and pressed his attention back to the books in front of him.

Chapter Nine

Cripples

It took a long time for her to reach a decision. After Haakie confirmed what Nina suspected from the gossip she had overhead, she locked herself in her one room, waiting, like Isabella, for some divine intervention in her tangled life.

She saw him once, from her window, as he passed on his way to the shop.

She kept low, peering through the break in the curtain. He looked so changed that she hardly recognised him. Age had crept up on Magnus as it had with her.

Haakie sent her a sailor, but she refused to open the door as the fist beat louder and louder. A foreign voice shouted, disturbing the peace of the night. She knew that ears would hear and that mouths would talk.

Tired of her existence she closed her mind to the noise. She was tired of love-making, of strange men, of being outcast. Her bloom was withered now, a pink rose browning at it's petal edges.

She ignored her appearance totally. Days passed in a dither of delusion.

Her hair knotted, her skin became sticky with the unwashed oils of her body. She didn't care.

She saw him once and that was enough. The senselessness of her self-pity became plain to her. Regrets would not help. But still she could not break out of the lethargic dwalm that afflicted her.

Finally, in a desperate attempt to outwit her confusion, she took a razor and opened the blade from the handle. She watched it entice her, the star of sunlight glinting along it's edge. She held it over the soft bangled wrist; the skin trembled, defenceless, like a crab's soft back out of its shell. She drew the blade across her wrist, making a thin superficial cut. Blood seeped out, tiny red globules. She dropped the razor, and wrapped the cut in a cloth. The blood seeped through it. It would not stop.

Terrified, she flung open the door of her house weeping, still holding the blood soaked cloth to her cut. She clattered down the steps out into the street screaming.

Doors opened, heads poked from windows. For a boundless minute, no one came. She fell to her knees in the middle of the street, sobbing.

"Help me. Please, somebody."

No one moved. For another fraction of eternity, she thought they would leave her to bleed to death, right there in the heart of Mirkwick, in full view of all.

Then she felt a hand on her. She felt herself lifted and carried. She gazed up into the face of her Samaritan, and saw it was the cripple.

He took her to her room, where he bathed the wound with hot water, and dressed it carefully. She was fevered, in a dreadful panic, not merely the result of the cut, but the product of the deep gash in her heart.

She poured her problems over him. He listened but was confused by it all. There was no rhyme or reason to it all.

He helped her to bed. He touched the soft skin that so many had caressed, and knew why she was so desired.

She slept for two days. Ertie called twice, bringing her food. He was extremely disturbed at the thought of her suicide attempt.

When she finally awoke, the fever had passed and she ate some of the food he had brought.

"Where did du get dis?" she asked him.

"I found some money here. I took nothing for myself, I swear."

He took a cloth and washed her face.

"You must promise not to try to take your own life again."

"I promise."

"You must not think badly of yourself, Nina. You have dignity like all. It is only for you to discover it."

She looked at him surprised. What did he know of dignity, poor cripple that he was, the butt of everyone's jokes?

He finished washing her face. He put the cloth in a basin by the bedside.

"My mother used to wash my face like that when I was ill," he said.

She turned on her pillow and faced the wall.

"Where does du come from? I ken du's a shipwrecked sailor, but . . ?

"I come from Italy. My name is Arturo. That is why they call me Ertie here, because it is like Arthur."

"Isn't it queer how life washes folk up? Not just dee, Arturo (she smiled thinking of his other secret name) but all o' wis."

She turned back to face him again.

"I truly do appreciate dy kindness."

He blushed.

"I could do no other. You gave me a coat."

She felt sad, thinking of the mood she had been in when she gave him that coat. An old ragged coat which she thought had been a kind of joke. Yet he had remembered all those years afterwards, as if he had treasured it.

He seemed to gauge her thoughts.

"No one gives me presents," he said.

Ertie called regularly through the next few days.

He would come and she would give him money, so they could eat. Then he would cook something simple for them, and together they laughed and ate in the lamplight. Then one night, when he had given her hot broth, she gripped his arm.

"I'm going awa'," she spoke sadly.

He took her empty bowl from her.

"The soup was good?" he asked.

"I said I'm going."

"I know. I thought you may."

She watched him wash the bowls out. He bent over the stove, his awkward hunched shape ragged and melancholy.

"How old is du, Arturo?"

"Forty and some more, I do not know."

"If I told dee I wanted dee to leave Mirkwick with me, what would du say?"

The question took him totally by surprise.

"I . . . " he stammered. "I am a cripple . . . . "

"Yes. I ken dat. But du's kind and good. It's a long time since I kent kindness."

"No, Nina, no. It is not enough . . . . "

She said no more then, but when next he came, she asked him again.

This time he cried with happiness.

"You are young and can make a new life. I have nothing left to offer you. Go yourself, and be happy."

She shook her head.

"No, come with me. We can go to Italy, and we will see your home, and . . "

He cut her short.

"That is a dream, Nina. I have no home but Mirkwick, I will die here."

Sadly she accepted this.

Her rest had helped her shed her sorrow and her shame. The name of Magnus Doull no longer caused her convulsions. She gathered together her few possessions in readiness for the steamer's visit on Tuesday.

Arturo wished her well.

"I am old. If I were younger. I might come with you. But you, you have a whole life to lead, and me, an old ragged cripple tagging along, no, no."

On Monday, about six o' clock in the evening, he came. She opened the door to him as if she expected him.

"Magnus."

"Nina."

He looked about the room where she lived, and caught sight of the little bag on the chair, and the empty drawers open.

"I'm going on da steamer da moarn," she confirmed.

"I ken. I heard. I wanted ta come afore, Nina, I did."

She turned away from him. Magnus watched her face in the mirror. Long gone images of youth and tender moments. The touch of her skin. Her dark eyes, girlish and uncertain.

"Things have changed dan, for both of wis," he said finally.

She was crying.

"Maybe if da bairn had lived."

"I ken. Meenie telt me."

She spun on her heel, and blinded by tears she walked straight into his bulk.

"Magnus. I've made up my mind. I'm going."

He wanted to reach out and embrace her.

"Will du go, please."

He took one look at her. The moment had passed. He had missed it.

Not knowing what to say, he tried to smile.

Through tears and tangled hair, she returned his look.

"Good luck dan."

When Arturo came to see her that night she was crying. But it was not the awful despair of a week ago.

She cried these tears for all the things she had wanted to say to Magnus but couldn't.

He had been in the room barely two minutes, and she had sent him away.

Everything that had been between them erased in two minutes of abrupt speech and buried in the words "Good Luck."

She smiled a bittersweet smile.

Arturo stroked her hair. She reached out to him, and he held her. Warmth passed between them. Suddenly she placed her lips on the cripple's. He pulled away, but she held him tight. Like a schoolgirl, he resisted, but she held him.

"I'm a cripple . . "

But it was her voice, not his, that whispered these words.

"A cripple like dee, in here."

She took his hand and placed it on the fullness of her breast.

"Feel it, Arturo, feel the ugliness."

"No, no, not ugliness, Nina. It is pure."

It was the last time that clandestine love sweated on the little bed above the store. In the morning Nina took her small case and went to the pier.

As the flit boat moved smoothly through the water, she looked back for the last time at Mirkwick. The Haa house, the shop, the Böd and the little stone house that had been her home. She sighed. This was ten years too late to leave. She had wasted time in the depths of self pity. But she would make the most of what was left to her. She had money. She would survive.

People were glad. Nina had really topped it all with her suicide attempt.

Screaming and weeping in the middle of the street and all.

But now she was gone. All would be well.

Ertie watched from the window of the smithy, broom in hand.

Andrew the smith was at the anvil.

"Come on Ertie, da fire's getting low," he called above the roar. Ertie moved back to the heat of the furnace.

In his nostrils there remained the wistful scent of perfume and love, intermingled. He would never forget her kindness to him.

Chapter Ten

Hairst Blinks

Expectations for the long winter seemed rosy. At Turmtillen the store of salted fish, and even a little pork, appeared more than adequate. The crops of tatties and neaps and kale were good.

And Magnus was rightly pleased with his summer's work on the croft. He had pointed up the old house with mortar, had repaired the thatched roof, and fitted a new door to help keep out the winter gales.

He should have been satisfied. Yet there was something wrong. Meenie sensed it as she watched him pace the floor frowning. His gaze flitted from one thing to another, agitated.

Perhaps it was Nina. She had heard from Bessie that she was leaving on the steamer that day. When Magnus wandered distractedly out of the house, saying he was going to the banks, she went to the old dresser and took the cards from the drawer.

It was with Magnus in mind that she laid the cards out in the ritual shape of the Celtic cross, as the tinkie had shown her.

The first card designated the subject of the reading. She placed it over the significator which represented Magnus. It showed his state of mind and the influences affecting them. It was the Knight of Rods — conflict and rivalry.

The chink of china, hot tea pouring from the spout of a brown earthenware pot. She crouched over the cards.

Their patterns repeat themselves, like the Fair Isle she knits with her wizened old hands; she recognises their seemingly random occurrence. And she has dreams, strange dreams, out of shape, in which she walks through the future unseen in a weird warped unbalanced dimension. Aald Meenie has the sight.

She laid the tenth card, and felt a shudder run through her old body. In the sixth place, was the Death Card. In the tenth, the final outcome, the Fool. The card is reversed.

It was a pattern she had never seen before, but it scared her. Her senses told her it forbade happiness, that it predicted sorrow and folly.

Meenie put the cards away. Although she did not understand, she knew better than to use their powers again. They would only confuse her more. She could only wait and hope that their meaning would be revealed to her in some other way.

Night came in a thick black cloak, enveloping the lands of Mirkwick in the devil's realm. Magnus still had not returned. Meenie, disturbed by the reading of the cards, went to bed but slept little. She waited for the sound of the latch being lifted. She dozed a little, rose twice to see if Magnus had returned while she slept, but six o'clock came crisp and new, and there was still no figure in the box-bed.

Meenie rose and poked among the embers of the peat fire smoking in the middle of the but end floor. She placed a couple of peats carefully to revitalise it. Fire, she thought, fire that burns continuously. It was considered poor housekeeping to let the flame go to its ashen remains.

Absentmindedly, she went to the door and looked out. Morning was coming out of the heavens, dizzy beams of cool sunlight spraying down from an invisible source in a low grey blanket of cloud.

She could see a few of the villagers already at their labours. The Johnsons were up early building a corn stook in the back yard. She watched for a while idly. It had been a tragedy, Ollie's death.

Her concentration slipped further away to the reading of the night before. The Death Card had appeared in the sixth place, the realm of the immediate future, and though its meaning was not necessarily death, she had a feeling that in this case it might well be so.

And the Fool in the tenth place? Who could it be that was about to be dealt with unfairly, to suffer severely for his folly?

After her morning tea, Meenie put on her hap, and went outside to attend to the croft work. She fetched peats from the stack, and fed the animals. Though disturbed by the cards, she could not forget the day to day routine.

A rook flew across her path and settled on the dyke at the side of the house. She spoke to it gently.

"Hello, Jocky boy."

She paced towards the rook on tiptoe. The woman fixed the bird in her hypnotic stare. It stepped from leg to leg nervously.

"Come noo Jocky, tell Aald Meenie whit du sees fae so high ida sky."

She moved closer.

"Tell me, Jocky, tell Aald Meenie."

The rook spread its wings, and with two heavy black beats it lifted from the dyke. Meenie watched as it flew far out over the voe. Then, as if caught by some current of air, it stopped, then soared through the air without moving its wings till it came above the pierhead. Meenie tried desperately to see where it landed, but she lost sight of it among the dark buildings. Then it reappeared in the sky and flew hard across the wick to Turmtillen. It landed where it had sat on the dyke.

"Thank you, Jocky boy," she said softly, "thank you," and she found in the pocket of her peenie a handful of corn puckles, which she threw to it.

A rush of thoughts passed through her head.

It was an omen all right. But what did it mean? How it all puzzled her! Still, she could do nothing about it. She went on with her chores, grim faced, her mind far away in that mysterious dimension of the future.

That rare and twinkling dawn had risen so peacefully, thin and elusive as if fashioned from the finest crystal, that the painter striving to capture it would have torn his hair out by the roots.

It was a purity heightened by its rarity, made more priceless by its infrequency.

Aald Seemon stopped his labours for a minute or two, and reflected on the calm of the elements. He pondered the vastness of it all, this creation that he was such a tiny part of. He was a wise old soul, Seemon Sinclair, and his wisdom was a direct result of his perception of infinity, and indeed of the infinitesimal. This is when he feels his religious need most satisfied, on mornings like these, days when the eye could see clear up to heaven were it but strong enough.

This inner joy the old man never shares. Not even with dear Bessie. It is alone, and he hasn't the words to share it. It is enough that he should feel it, for then he goes about his daily work with the joy inside his easy soul renewed, the purpose of his bare existence revealed to him. He knows the fallacy of regret and memory, yet enjoys both the past and the present equally. For though he lovingly caresses all his past with hands that fear to break the image, he knows that there is no effective way to turn the clock back, or to sign a pact with Time to guarantee it motionless.

Seemon leans his elbow on a dyke, taps his pipe to clear the bowl, and puts it in his breast pocket where it sticks out like a carnation. He feels no sorrow at the passing of Time, will never try to stop his clock and live in youth forever. He has reached that period of life when action gives way to meandering thought, that wonderful time before death when a person has time to look back without regret at all that they have done.

Seemon feels no sorrow at the passing of time. He knows that age is as natural as morning following night, and never questions.

And Magnus Doull, alone on the clifftop at Crugness has spent the whole night thinking of the irrefutable nature of Time as he too watches daylight scorn the dark.

Day becomes night, and night flows into day.

He waited all night for the first sign of dawn. When it came he missed it. There was no one moment when day began. The blue of the dark became lighter and lighter till the cerulean transformed into pinks and lemons and roseate sweeps. Then the sun appeared, fresh and new. A man should see the sunrise every so often. The soul responds. This was Magnus' god, this chariot of fire charming the sky. He monitored morning from the clifftop in a state of meditation.

She had gone. He had watched as the steamer sailed past, bound for Lerwick, its calls complete. He knew she was on board.

Youthful artless lovers they had been, neither knowing how to please the other, yet there existed between them some elemental desire which lifted them to the peak of ecstasy. That first time after the Roup, when he was drunk with his first taste of whisky, and she barefoot. How they had run to the byre at Shalderwick, where it was empty and quiet, and the hay was dry. And that fine night when they had bathed naked in the moonlight at Dilse Geo, the numbing water tightening young skin over stiff muscles.

This stolen love was far sweeter than even the honey

of the Orient he had paid to taste in Bangkok, and far more bitter now that he had lost it.

Yet as he watched the daylight die and sleep and live again, so he knew that it was all a part of some pattern that he could not understand. A complex web of occurrence which formed the skeleton of his life.

She was further from him now than she had ever been during his time away. At least then he had retained some hope. Now that too was gone. The brief encounter in her empty room had wiped all from his mind. It was as they said. She was a whore.

Yet he couldn't prevent himself from speculating that if he'd only managed to reach out to her and touch her once, if he might not have awakened in her some sleeping love that had left her when he did.

Magnus had come to the cliffs at Crugness as a boy whenever he needed to be alone. Here the crashing seas below had soothed his growing anger and frustration. The vast impenetrable blue seemed to suck the pain from him and leave him whole.

Memories of his boyhood flickered in his mind. He thought of Meenie and her potions, her undying faith in the old arts her mother had taught her, and her skill of prediction with her cards.

And he thought of his father, and of the things that had never been said between them. Magnus had been too young and too preoccupied with himself, to stop and realise that his father was but a man with the same longing for love as the rest of creation. Oh the fights they had had, as Magnus grew up. And now the time had long syne passed when the right words could be spoken.

Magnus tried to imagine the grave and how it must feel to the decaying flesh, if indeed it felt at all. He had never devoted much thought to Death, not even when he saw the pallid grey-blue face of his father nailed forever beneath the coffin lid.

Here on the cliff top he sat the whole night. He

listened to sounds of a life beyond human comprehension, the sea and the creatures taking sustenance from it. He wondered at the intricacy of its planning. Larger eats smaller, to be eaten in turn by larger still. In all this he observed a pattern not unlike those of Meenie's cards.

Yet one thing puzzled him. While Nature designated existence with apparent fairness, Mankind wanted more. He wanted everything, the whole planet. And as he listened to the cries of the birds awakening, as he watched them fly past him, so close that he could almost touch them, he listened to the sounds they made, their swoops and wails and squawks.

He mimicked their calls and returned them to the birds. The cries became louder and more widespread, as other birds joined in, maalies, blackbacks, tirricks and shalders.

He fancied he understood the meaning of their calls, that they were limited in their communicative powers to such an extent that his own imitation of their sounds confused them.

And he thought that this was the secret of Man's victory in the evolutionary race. He was the most complete mimic, could communicate with all creatures in their tongues, using their sounds to master them.

Mankind, the perfect mimic, the secret of his power!

Magnus laughed. He laughed so loud that the birds grew still more agitated and flapped and and squawked still more animatedly. The sound of his amusement echoed around the cliffs, the silence of Nature split by his guffaws.

And as he laughed the weight that had troubled him lifted. The louder he laughed the easier the burden became.

Magnus at last let the ghost of his father decay with his flesh. For years he had held onto irrational thoughts. He was seventeen when the old man died, and the memory of the day when the Haaf fishermen found him drifting about in his beloved boat out beyond Hulterness had long haunted him. It was the old man's heart that had given in. He couldn't relax, even after he left the fishing. It was as if he felt he had to show everybody in Mirkwick that his family were like everyone else, as if he had to work in full view of the gossips to show that Meenie and Magnus were not odd, as if he had to make up for their oddity.

Like so many of his kin, he had worked hard all his life and didn't know any other way of existing.

They say that the land a man lives on colours his character in the same certain way that the sea winds will tan his face. As the north gales blow, and the driftwood rides the waves to the shore, you might look out your window and see the old crofter collecting the drift and the sea-worn treetrunks that have been carried from some distant place. Watch as he makes neat piles of his loot under the banks, head bent into the wind, holding his pipe firmly between his teeth. Speechless he goes, with slow determined movement, unaware and uncaring of your gaze. And as you watch you realise that here is the creature most suited to survival in this harsh merciless climate.

But their's is the lot of slaves, their lives traded for meagre survival, until like Magnus Doull's father they die of overwork.

What keeps them in this inhospitable place, harnessed in this yoke of slavery?

Why simply that they are who they are, that they are born to this existence. And hard though it may be, it is rewarding in a way that no slave of the industrial revolution is rewarded. No gadgets to furnish the home, maybe, other than those that ingenuity devises, but every day provides a fresh challenge and requires creative thought to overcome it.

The crofter repairs his house with wood from the sea,

catches and grows his own food. He decides what he will do each day, no factory whistle to punctuate his life.

It is an impoverished life, yet it is rich. It is a hungry life, yet it is full. Races of people, living in an environment grow in tune with it. This treeless mesmerising landscape has given birth to a peculiar hardiness, a reliance on their basic trust in Creation, able to explain even the most terrifying phenomena with a brief sour spit of tobacco and a wise seafaring gesture to the ocean and its waywardness.

Wise and unflustered in death, wise and unflustered in birth. These are a well designed breed, their pedigree variant in the varying degrees of their independence from the outside world.

Aald Seemon went back to work in the corn.

"Tea an' salt," he grinned.

"Dat's aa' we buy an' we pay for dat we wir eggs."

Two separate men, in similar experience and thought returned to their homes as a summer storm began. Thunder rumbled as lightning flashed across the sky. Rain lashed down briefly, stiff and severe.

Seemon ducked into the but-room. Bessie poured him a cup of tea. Meenie saw Magnus return, as she weeded her neaps. She saw a smile on his face.

"Fine morning," she smiled, her heart lightened, "Hairst blinks though I see . . ."

"Ja, dat's da way o' it."

Meenie crossed off one possibility from her list of possible disasters. It had been troubling her ever since Magnus had left the croft the previous night.

He entered the crofthouse just ahead of her, and suddenly turned and gave her a warm smile.

She touched his shoulder fondly.

But she was still no nearer understanding.

Chapter Eleven

The Course of Investigation

The Reverend Cunningham and accompanying stranger were shown into the reception room at the Haa.

The stranger was small, slightly balding, with a large bushy moustache. He was an officious looking man, and was obviously not from Mirkwick by the well-tailored suit and the sharp nature of his expresssion. He was clearly a town dweller.

The laird ambled into the reception room. He looked in good humour, thought the minister, and he moved quickly across the room to shake the landowner's hand.

The laird was dressed in a thick tweed suit which disguised his portly figure. He shook the minister's hand loosely.

"Good morning," the Reverend Cunningham sang.

"Good morning." The reply was distracted, even uninterested.

The minister noticed this lack of conviction.

"This is Mr More," he said, as the stranger moved forward and gripped the laird's hand in turn.

"He's the special constable assigned to the murder case here."

The laird looked surprised.

"A murder, you say? Why haven't I heard anything of this before?"

The minister laughed.

"But you have! A long time ago, ten years now."

The laird sat down in one of the leather armchairs and gestured to the others to do likewise.

"Ten years, you say? Seems a bit late to do the investigating. What kept you, Mr More, did someone steal a loaf of bread in Lerwick?"

This was not well received by the policeman, who glared at the laird.

"We'd have done our job, sir, if people of the district had done their's. Your own rancelmen are to blame, I think."

The laird was unaccustommed to meeting people who were not in awe of his social position. More's bearing annoyed him, and he silently resolved not to help this man futher than decorum necessitated.

"So what's to be done now, ten years afterwards?" he queried, uncertain of the facts of the murder, but not wishing to disclose this to the policeman.

The special constable, his round and wrinkled moustachioed face creasing as he saw the opportunity to play the dectective, leaned back in the cockpit armchair, and twisted the corner of his moustache with a well-practised action.

"The truth, sir, we only want to know the truth. If the man is guilty, then he'll be punished as the court sees fit, if not, then I'll have done my job regardless. But the truth, sir, the truth will out. I'll be here in Mirkwick until that day if it takes me a month."

The laird postulated it might take much longer due to the time elapsed.

"You'll find the people have short memories, I think. What's past is past to them."

More frowned.

"If by that you mean that there may be information

concealed, then I'll make it plain now that I will punish that offence by the appropriate charge.''

The laird, fresh from the library where he had been continuing his Bible studies under the direction of Ellen Mitchell, thought this fellow the most meddlesome impertinent man he had met in many a year. His original resolution was confirmed in his mind, not merely to do no more than necessary, but to actively hinder this policeman if at all possible.

The Reverend Cunningham cut into the conversation.

''I'm sure there will be no need for that. We all want to know the truth. If the man is a murderer, then we all wish to see him punished. This is a Christian community, Mr More, and you'll see that we support justice.''

The laird took his cue from the minister's searching look.

''Of course, I'll do everything I can.''

More realised that the laird would be of little help. The policeman suspected that the laird resented this intrusion by the powers of law and order into his community, and in this he may have been right. Only the minister was left feeling that more could have been said, both by the laird whom he thought most unforthcoming, and by the policeman, whom Robert Williamson and himself had secretly sent for without telling even the good parishioners.

The arrival of the policeman was greeted by the villagers with apprehension. He rooted about those first few days asking questions, and the folk did not take to his probing personality. As the laird had suggested, they helped his investigation as little as possible.

Of course, there were some who were glad of his presence.

Mrs Williamson who had volunteered to give the man lodgings while he remained in the parish, was one. She thought this an honour, and she fluttered about, fussing over her guest, who took every drop of hospitality offered him, and responded to her "other" attentions by waxing his moustache.

"It's something about moustaches," she thought as she dabbed perfume carefully behind her ears before dinner, "It must be."

Robert Williamson was pleased at first to have the important visitor as a houseguest, but as he was made painfully aware of his wife's unsubtle flirtations, he became annoyed. Tightlipped, he retired to his office in the shop whenever possible, making the excuse that he had the accounts to prepare.

"Post Office, you'll understand," he disclosed.

The policeman nodded. He understood officialdom.

Robert gave his wife the stage on which to make a fool of herself if she so wished. Mrs Williamson revelled in this freedom.

She thought hard about any information she could give the "detective", as she called him, and described from her intimate knowledge of other people's affairs the character and standing of every member of the community. What she didn't know, she filled in with her imagination.

More listened carefully to all this. He thought to himself, as he poured yet another glass of the shop-keeper's brandy, that he had stumbled on a nice cosy refuge from work for a while, and he intended to spin it out for as long as possible. It wasn't often he had a murder with which to swell his self-importance . . .

A week passed, and after the first two days he never left the house next to the shop.

The course of investigation then, hardly went as the minister and Mr Williamson had intended it should. The minister was particularly disturbed, as he had Isabella at him every day, asking how things were going, and when would they hang him. It nagged at him that he should have nothing to tell her, so finally he went one day to the house next to the shop to have it out with the policeman, and presented himself at the front door.

Mrs Williamson thought to herself that the minister was in a strange mood, as she went to make the two men a pot of tea. So in the midst of her flutterings of the heart was she, that she thought nothing of the minister finding her darning a pair of More's socks, and sitting so close to him that she was almost on his knee.

As she returned with a tray of home-bakes, she heard the voices talking angrily.

"But you haven't even been to question Doull yet? What kind of an investigation is that? Mark my words there'll be a report."

This last word seemed to ring a bell under the bald skull of the policeman. It brought him back to earth and he assumed the identity of the detective again.

"My dear sir," he began, the smile gone from his face, "I have been doing some very important groundwork here. Mrs Williamson possesses an excellent knowledge of the community and its affairs, and any policeman worth his salt will tell you that it is vital to gain a sound overall picture before beginning detailed investigation. She has been kind enough to give me the benefit of her advice and assistance, and I will soon begin detailed inquiries as you suggest."

The minister felt more than a little stupid.

He made his excuses and left, just as Mrs Williamson appeared with her tray. Although he had made a fool of himself with the policeman, at least he would have something to tell Isabella now.

"Won't you have a cup of tea?" offered the hostess, but he had gone before she finished speaking.

"Well, you'll have a cup at least, won't you John?" she beamed.

"No, no, thank you."

More went to his room. He couldn't afford to have

his name besmirched by a bad report to headquarters. The flirtation would have to stop.

He waited a couple of days to allay the minister's suspicions, then set out one morning across the now shorn fields of early winter, in the direction of Turmtillen.

No one else but Seemon had risen. He watched the policeman go, and shook his head. Magnus had a fearful temper.

In Turmtillen, two heads slept at rest. They had not left the croft since the policeman's arrival, and so were not aware of his presence in Mirkwick.

Chapter Twelve

Aald Meenie's Eye

When Meenie slipped quietly out of the crofthouse, closing the new door behind her, the morning was damp and dewy still.

Magnus was asleep, and she had no inclination to rouse him. He had been working late into the night on a new gate for the yard.

She went to the byre and was about to enter when the birds suddenly took up a singing that so startled her that she put down the paid of fodder she was taking to the hens, and listened.

She was astonished to hear them. They sang quite plainly of a stranger roaming about, whose intent was evil. Meenie listened to the bird song, to the message they gave her. She knew that all these strange phenomena were related, and put this warning with the omen the rook had brought her, and the reading of the cards.

The birds repeated their messages four times and then were silent. Meenie threw a handful of corn from her pail, as a reward for their confidence.

She went into the byre, and set down the hen's feeding. The smell of dung and straw and bovine birth filled the byre, for the old cow had not long since given birth to a bull calf.

It was a disappointment, for Meenie would dearly have liked a second milker now that Magnus was back, and she felt this to be a setback to the process of rejuvenation taking place at Turmtillen. Still, there would be a bit of veal for them to eat, and Meenie was wise enough to know that nothing happened that did not have some use in life.

She saw to the cows needs and sat for a while on an old upturned kettle in the gjiurm of the byre, playing with the young calf, teasing it. The old cow watched wary, but she trusted Meenie.

Taking the pail of feeding for the hens, Meenie emerged from the gloom of the byre, and it was then that she saw the stranger. He was coming walking up through the parks to Turmtillen. Evil should be met head on, Meenie believed, and she waited pail in hand until the stranger reached her.

Five years ago, the ladies of the village had for some reason decided that Meenie was in need of their assistance, and a group of them arrived at Turmtillen one day, armed with good intentions and Christian thoughts.

Meenie met them head on, when they had turned their interfering eyes on her.

"Ging awa' ," she told them, quite plainly to their faces, "You caa' me a witch ahint my back, an' come ta me when you're ill. You're aa' hypocrites, though half o' you are dat stupid you'll no ken whit dat is."

The ladies of the mission excused their embarrassment to each other by agreeing that Meenie was crazy. They also agreed that something should be done about it but as usual nothing was. In truth they were all individually afraid of Meenie and her powers, and stayed as far away from her as possible.

No, Meenie did not hide away from evil intent, and she stood her ground as the stranger approached. He walked right up to her, silently, till he stood not a step from her face.

Meenie fixed him with her one good eye.

"Is this the residence of Magnus Doull, Seaman?" he asked in his officious manner.

Meenie nodded.

The policeman tried to avoid shuffling his feet, but Meenie's glare disconcerted him. He felt as if that cyclops face were burning a bullet hole through him.

"My name is More. I've been appointed special investigator to a murder case. The case of one Thomas Pole."

He said this with an attempt at a penetrating glance, but he looked straight at the skin-covered eye of Meenie, and his attempt failed.

"And whit his dis to do wi' my Magnus?"

The investigator winced.

"A few questions, Mrs Doull, you are Mrs Doull, aren't you?"

"Aye."

Meenie kept him secured in her vision for a few seconds, during which time she mastered his evil.

Then she turned, and walked towards the croft-house.

"I'll git him, dan."

But Magnus had heard the voices, and he came out to see who this was, his trousers pulled on crumpled, his braces about his knees.

"And who might dis be, midder?," he asked, he too sensing the aura of the policeman.

Magnus' eyes were near as potent as his mother's, staring at the man from under a wild mop of red hair, his jaw set aggressively under the beard.

"More," said the investigator, "Special constable More. I've been assigned to the case of the murder of Thomas Pole. I believe you knew him?"

Magnus and Meenie side by side were a powerful force, and More felt it.

"I kent him."

"You knew about his murder?"

Magnus said nothing. More took this to mean that

he was getting through to Doull, and continued to probe.

"And I have heard that you ran away because you were guilty."

These accusations were facts that both Magnus and Meenie knew, but they had fallen into the habit of forgetting them. They never alluded to them, and to hear them spoken suddenly stirred their hidden anger.

Magnus leapt forward to push his face into More's.

"It wis ten years ago. Can you no' forget it?" he bellowed.

This outburst seemed to calm him. He retreated to Meenie's side, fiery red.

More was visibly shaken. He said nothing but watched Doull with a look of disguised fear.

"I will warn you now that I am carrying a pistol," he said in an effort at a level tone.

"And I will warn you that if you are not beyond that dyke before I lose my temper that I will break your bloody neck!"

More twitched. He was uncertain whether to run or to bluff.

He decided to try another approach.

"Come, come, we're talking like hooligans. I just require the answers to a few questions."

"Questions, aye questions," shouted Magnus, "Questions that'll lead to the gallows for me, guilty or not. I ken your justice. I've seen justice in a thousand different ports, I ken," he yelled, still full of fire.

"Not at all, Mr Doull, we're as keen to determine your innocence as anything else. But you do understand this has to be cleared up. It can't remain a blot on our copybook forever. While you were away we weren't able to determine anything. You do understand?" More sneered an effort at a confidential smile.

Magnus stood silent, eyelids flickering, as if thinking furiously.

Then he rushed forward at the little detective like a

bull, and picked him up before the man had time to extract his pistol from its hidden holster. Magnus ran down over the toons with him in his iron grip, and dumped the fellow over the dyke on the land of the next croft, at Shalderwick.

The special constable struggled to find his gun, but discovered to his horror that it had fallen from his person.

Magnus stood panting, his red hair blowing frantically in the wind.

"I'll take this as an admission of guilt, Doull," spat the policeman. "And I'll find the evidence, damn me if I don't. I was prepared to give you a chance to explain yourself but not now. I'll see you hang, Doull, damn me if I don't."

With that, he got to his feet, and straightened his garments, and started to walk for the safety of Mrs Williamson's ben-end.

He decided to leave the gun, but resolved to arrest Doull on a charge of theft if nothing else. That made him feel better. He could do that. After all he was a special constable.

Chapter Thirteen

Rum Stories

Haakie Manson refilled Seemon's glass.

They were alone in the tavern.

"Dey say he's a changed man, Haakie continued.

"And wha'd a thought it?" Seemon answered. "Da aald buggar'd been yon way since da day he wis born, as far as I ken.

Seemon flicked a coin onto the counter, but Haakie pushed it back to him.

"Aye, it's a surprise indeed. Wha'd a thought a slip o' a lass could have an effect like dat on a grown man."

Haakie didn't generally drink when he was behind the bar, but when Seemon came in it was different. He sipped from a full glass of rum.

"Reading da Bible indeed. I always thought he got his inspiration fae da Mellishon itsel'."

They both roared and laughed at Haakie's observation.

The change in the laird's habits was the subject on the parish tongue at the moment. At first, no one had taken the news seriously, but as further reports filtered through from the hidden world inside the Haa walls, they were forced to believe that it was a changed place since Ellen's arrival.

"And whit about dis detective fellow? Has du heard ought a' him lately?"

Haakie swallowed his gulp of rum. He shook his head.

"He's been awa' dis past week. Took da steamer ta Lerwick on Tuesday."

Seemon expressed surprise at this.

"Surely he's no' given up already? He seemed a bit of a ferret to me. I didna reckon on him given up so readily."

Haakie lit a small cigarillo.

"No, he'll be back. In fact he made a point of telling me he wid. He's up to something, dat wan. Magnus had better watch himsel', or he'll find himsel' on da end of a very short rope."

This they agreed on. The story of the special constable's visit to Turmtillen had not yet leaked. Only More himself and the Turmtillen folk were in a position to reveal it, and Magnus and Meenie had not yet left the house. More had no intentions of undermining his repect by recounting his embarrassment.

"It's a bad thing for aa'body really," said Seemon frowning.

"Whit is?" asked Haakie.

"Dis whole business. Tammas Pole. Dey'd have been better to let it lie."

Haakie agreed.

"It's upsetting aa'body," he confirmed. "We can do aa'thoot folk coming poking der noses into da past, digging up Guid kens whit."

They talked a bit more about this and that, saying little really, but enjoying themselves immensely. The rum bottle emptied, and no coins entered the till. This was a social occasion for Haakie, not business.

When he finally said cheerio to Seemon, he was well oiled, as he put it, and flopped down into one of the seats. He mopped his head with his apron, and began to drift into a light sleep.

Thoughts fled through his head at a terrific speed.

Haakie did a lot of talking in the course of a day's work, and it was fine to be able to close his mouth for a while, and let the brain sort out all the information he had gleaned. In his position at the pierhead, he was able to control the parish tongue quite effectively, and often Haakie's opinions might be heard on one of the outlying crofts months after he had expressed it.

He was always well informed.

Haakie started as the alehouse door creaked open. He jumped to his feet, refreshed by his brief respite, and was ready to engage in another conversation.

It was Thomas Sutherland, the factor.

"Good day, Tammas," said Haakie, welcoming.

"Is it?" asked Sutherland, looking dejected.

"Rum, Haakie, a muckle wan."

Haakie obliged, and poured himself one too, as his mouth felt a little furry after his short sleep.

"Du's awful doon in da mooth," he observed.

The factor drank back his glass and pushed it forward for another.

He didn't reply.

"We've been hearing strange tales about da laird," said Haakie fishing.

"Dey say he's been converted," he probed, watching the factor's reaction.

"Wha says?" Sutherland asked, looking at the publican quizically.

"Och, a few different sources. Dey say it's yon Miss Mitchell that's brought it about. A powerful faith she must have, to convert da Aald Fellow."

Sutherland wasn't amused.

"Whit else have dey been saying about her?" he asked.

Haakie sensed his displeasure.

"Och, nothing. Dey say she's a fine lass."

"And so she is," replied Sutherland angrily. "Far too good for her name to be spoken by dy fishwife's lips." And with that he left the alehouse in a flame.

"Oy, du's no paid," called out Haakie, but he was away.

Haakie put the financial loss out of his mind. He smiled.

The fishwife in him detected a sorely troubled soul.

It would not be long before the factor's ailments were common knowledge. Haakie would see to that. He'd had a strong dislike of Thomas Sutherland, which went a long way back. He wasn't the man he pretended to be, Haakie knew. He had heard tell of his doings and didn't like what he heard.

In his younger days, Sutherland had been a pleasant enought fellow, always up for a gaff. But this job had changed him. He'd become sleekit, like all who have power, and his methods didn't always bear scrutiny.

Haakie had helped him out of jams before, and had received no thanks for it. He wouldn't do the same again, not in a hurry.

Chapter Fourteen

The Poison's Cure

Magnus' outburst of pent-up aggression had frightened Meenie.

She felt that it perhaps fitted the pattern being revealed to her. He was not cured of his temper, and it could yet prove the undoing of him. Magnus had made a powerful enemy, a man who despite his personal weakness had the powers of so-called law and justice behind him.

Magnus' calm state of mind disturbed, he turned again to his old refuge, the bottle. Into the doubts and fears that still hung over him, despite the ten years that had elapsed.

He thought it worse not to know if he was guilty, than to know for certain that he was. If he knew that he had killed Tammas Pole in a fit of drunken anger, then at least he could reconcile himself to that fact. But as long as the memory block persisted in his brain, the uncertainty gnawed away at his peace of mind, and he was not his own master. At any time he might encounter men like the policeman, More, and at any time he might be snared by their guile, trapped and hung, and he still not knowing whether he was justly punished or the victim of their cunning.

Meenie watched him grow more and more tense. He paced the floor and muttered to himself, and there was nothing she could do. She tried to penetrate his mind but he met her with confused looks and abstract words. She could only hope that her sixth sense would reveal something to her that could help to save him, yet even that power seemed to desert her as she found it impossible to decipher the messages it brought to her.

Turmtillen was a sadly troubled house since the visit of the special constable.

Magnus took the bottle from the press. He left the house, and walked up over the toons behind the croft until he came to the deserted clifftop at Crugness. The place where he had spent many an hour as a boy, and a place that he had always felt to be his.

Feet rarely walked these hills, he told himself. This was virgin soil beneath his feet. Possibly that last sod had not been stepped on since the days of the Broch-dwellers. It was good to know that there was still some earth unspoilt by Mankind, somewhere on this planet.

He bit the cork from the green bottle and spat it far away.

He would have no further need of it. He would drink until the last drop trickled down his open throat, confusing his body and mind until he was full of the poison.

He would bring himself to the point of death, and then wander back. And having seen death, there would be no unknown future, nothing that those self-righteous hypocrites and officious policemen could do to him. He would drink until he had putrified his dream in order to purify it.

His dream!

Had he really believed that he could return to Mirkwick as if the past had never happened? Did he really expect the people to forget? That was not the way of the world. There were those who loved to dig the dirt, like hens clucking and scraping, uncovering titbits to gobble up, to keep the very life in their bodies. There were people like hens all right, who thrived on the rotten things they discovered beneath the surface of the earth. The surface of life.

His bitterness, partly soothed by the first few months at Turmtillen, returned full scale, as horribly warped as ever.

He thought that he might as well give himself into their hands and give up this hopeless struggle to live a normal life again. It seemed that even his life of drunkenness and debauchery aboard ship had been preferrable to this; this uncertainty, this constant threat hanging over him. At least at sea he had been able to veil the past from his conscious mind. Now it was thrown up into his face every time he raised his eyes and looked beyond the dykes of Turmtillen.

Ah Whisky!

He drank thirstily, like a man intent on self-destruction, and this was not far from his mind as he sat on the clifftop with the wind blowing cold and damp about him. He could roll forward from the knoll he sat on, and he would be over the edge before he knew it, carried there by his own momentum. It seemed a comforting option to have in his frenzied state of mind.

Magnus drank until the flagon was empty, all the while his heart full of bitterness for the rest of Mankind. Life should be such a wonderful experience. Each day should be a glimpse of Paradise, could be an excursion to Heaven, followed by the fitful rest of a man living to the rhythms of his spirit.

But so few ever come to know that peace, that sense of purpose. They were all too busy trying to build an easier life. Progress, they cry, progress at all costs, until the day comes when there is nothing left for people to do, no challenge, so mechanised the world will have become. And people will spend their time squabbling and fighting out of boredom, till they bring about the destruction of everything they strived for centuries to build.

He could see traces of this future all around him. Mankind busy conquering Nature, not realising that in so doing they take the very essence of themselves and submit it to slavery. The very qualities that caused our evolutionary process to accelerate, now buried under the weight of slavery to the god of progress.

For we are all animals, highly-evolved granted, but still retaining our basic needs, to hunt, to eat, to sleep, to reproduce. How long will it take for Mankind to realise that the animal in us is far more noble and poetic than the God-like postures we assume? Will he ever realise?

But as Magnus looked about him at the land of Mirkwick, he knew that there was still hope. In men like Seemon, there was a glimmer of true contentment, in the tough crofting life, a glimpse of independence and a true challenge.

But with the oppressive forces of the Laird, penetrating the material, and the Kirk the spiritual, even here in this outpost of civilisation were the temples of the evils. The potential for contentment here in Mirkwick was wrapped in a cloak of darkness.

Large families, insufficient food. Poor homes, and no equipment with which to improve the land.

The perfect world in Magnus' mind would be where there was no poverty, not of the material or the spiritual, where men behaved as men, with dignity, where all had their basic rights, to decide the kind of life they would lead, free from the upper classes boxing them off into economic units, giving them a space and instructing them to fit into it.

But his anarchic heart was a prisoner itself, of that one night long ago and he couldn't see a way to free it. They would never leave him alone to build the life that lay before him, free and challenging. And then it struck him!

The only way was to fight. It was something he knew how to do, a trade that he had learned in the tough school before the mast, where men got drunk and killed with alarming regularity. He wasn't going to run away again. He had come back to see it finished with, and that was exactly what he would do.

Head spinning wildly from the whisky, Magnus lurched dangerously near to the cliff edge, as he stood up. In the nick of time he managed to find his balance, and he stared down to the rocks below, where the sea churned green, and showed its white teeth to the rock face. "Not yet," he breathed.

"Death?" he grinned, "death is just life inverted. They can't hurt me, nothing can." He clenched his fists in preperation for the forthcoming battle.

He was close to Death every instant that he lived, with the shadow of the gallows hanging over him. He would fight the system he hated, and if he died, then it would be no more than a repayment for the life of Tammas Pole. To believe himself a murderer! That was the secret. If he at last admitted to his secret heart that he was guilty then he could not be harmed. That knowledge would become his strength, and he would use it anyway he could, until they caught him as they inevitably must. But he'd give them a battle first. He wouldn't wait for them to come to him. He'd face their malice as Meenie did.

And if he were found not guilty, which seemed unlikely after his tangle with the policeman, then so much the better.

Oh the fires of whisky! What thoughts they burn into a man's brain! What transient strength they give!

Magnus Doull, poor tortured soul that he was, placed his faith in the powers of the liquor. But even in the midst of this misguided trust, a seed was sown that was not the child of Alcohol, but the birth of a new strength that was Magnus' creation.

He fell to his knees exhausted, his head intoxicated, his nervous system full of the poison, and slept, dreamless.

The birds swooped and squawked about him. The sea crashed into the rocks below, eating away at the cliffs with its white teeth. Magnus slept. Hours passed and when he eventually awoke, night had descended, and his clothes were wet with dew and drizzle.

He shivered. His head beat with a frantic pulse.

All was still. For a moment, he wondered if he might be dead, so empty was that instant of all sensual impression.

Gradually he pieced together the events of his fulminated drunkenness.

The powers given to his will by the whisky had gone, leaving only the traces of its illusion behind. But in Magnus' heart, the seed that had been sown was growing.

He *would* fight them. He *would* meet evil face to face.

And he would do it alone without alcohol.

He was strong, he didn't need bolstering.

Head aching, stomach churning, limbs lifeless, he staggered to the cliff edge, and cast the empty flagon from his hand. He watched it drop till it disappeared into the darkness hidden from the moonlight. Then he heard it crash on the rocks.

His mind was working quickly, planning it's strategy. Everything fitted. It was all possible.

Chapter Fifteen

Muskets Primed

The special constable returned on the steamer next Tuesday. He was wearing a new suit, as sharp as the first had been, and in his pocket holster he carried a new pistol; in his hand, a small wooden case with brass fittings.

The attention of the waiting villagers fell on his box. Curiosity murmured amongst them. The policeman was aware of the stir he caused, and he swelled his chest out to appear still more important.

He walked briskly up the pier and went into Haakie Manson's alehouse. Aald Seemon was enjoying his rum, leaning over the counter, whispering something in Haakie's ear when he entered, clearing his throat to attract attention.

Seemon turned to look at the special constable.

"Welcome back, Mr More," he said, and went back to the publican's ear. The policeman moved closer to try to overhear, afraid perhaps that the story of his encounter with Magnus Doull had leaked while he was away.

But Seemon stopped his disclosure before More was in earshot.

Haakie stretched himself.

"Whit'll it be, dan?"

The special constable shook his head.

"Oh, I'm not here socially," he said.

Both Haakie and Seemon looked at him with new interest.

"And whit is it dat brings you here, dan?"

Smugly, the policeman laid his case on the counter, revelling in the role of spy. He opened the brass lock on the case with a small key, and swung the lid back..

"Now I won't ask you if you've seen the like of this before because I know you haven't. It's a brand new technique, developed in India, and just adopted by the police force in England. By virtue of my connections within the force, I obtained this while I was away. I believe that it will help me solve the case of Thomas Pole's murder."

The two friends examined the contents of the case. To them it meant nothing. Magnifying glasses, small brass tins of powder, other unfamiliar items.

More waited until the two men were entirely baffled.

"Unusual, isn't it?" he said, his expression like that of a child showing off its new toy.

"And whit is dis conglomeration, pray tell?" asked Seemon, tired of the detective's game.

The detective picked up the magnifying glass, and peered through it.

"You two gentlemen might not be aware of this, but it seems that every man/woman or child alive has a very unique signature that no pen writes, but which is left wherever that individual may go. On everything they touch, as a matter of fact."

Haakie and Seemon looked at each other incredulously.

"No," sneered the policeman, "I am not delirious. Merely the possessor of some very priveleged information. As I said, I have connections. This technique of deciphering this 'signature' as I put it, is called 'Fingerprinting'."

He put down the magnifying glass and took hold of

Haakie's hand. Then, picking up the glass again, he positioned it above Haakie's fingers so as to magnify the tips.

"There," he said. "Look at that, look at the patterns of the skin through the glass."

This they did.

"Those patterns are entirely unique to the individual. No other living soul has the same patterns. And what's more, those patterns are left on everything the individual touches. Especially on smooth surfaces such as a glass."

"You see," he continued, "among the paraphenalia relating to this case I found at Headquarters, I found a broken bottle that had been in Pole's hand when he died. Some clever fellow had picked it up, not realising the significance it would later assume. And on that bottle, I found two sets of fingerprints. One I believe to have belonged to the dead man, the other . . . Well, more than likely, these were the murderer's. Doull's, I expect."

Haakie and Seemon listened stone-faced.

"So you mean you can prove Doull's guilty?" asked Seemon.

"That remains to be seen," the special investigator answered, but there was a smug self-confidence in his voice.

"And if da hands dat held da bottle were Magnus', will dat hang him?" Haakie asked, sneering, as if dubious of the truth of the policeman's story. He refilled Seemon's glass and his own.

"That is for the court to decide," said More, "but it will certainly be important evidence. Incontrovertible evidence that he was present the night that Pole died."

With that he closed his magic box, and bade them Good Day.

The two drinking pals looked at each other.

"Man, dat's a proper ferret, dat wan," said Seemon.

Haakie wasn't listening. He was thinking about what the policeman had said.

"It's a trick," he said. "He's trying to panic Magnus. He's telt wis so as we'll spread it aboot, so Magnus will hear about it, and give himsel' awa'."

Seemon was impressed by Haakie's reasoning.

"Du could easy be right," he said nodding his head.

They emptied their glasses again, and agreed to say nothing about it.

That was quite a vow for Haakie to take. He had never kept a secret in his life, so far as Seemon knew. But the dislike that the policeman was arousing in the parish was so intense that it had even reached the normally lucid mouth of the publican.

They began to laugh at having been taken in by the detective's story at first.

"Imagine it," roared Haakie, "hanged because o'da shape o' his fingers. Wha ever heard da like?"

"Du has to hand it to him, though," laughed Seemon, "he nearly had wis believing him."

Despite their resolution, the story of the fingerprinting did leak out. Though not as More had intended. It became the subject of derision about the parish, and when More went into the shop the following day to buy some tobacco, he couldn't understand why everyone looked at him with a smirk on their faces. The fingerprinting story was supposed to unsettle everyone, and here it seemed to have had the opposite effect. Maybe they had heard of his meeting with Magnus Doull and the thump he had received to his pride.

Only the Reverend Cunningham took the fingerprinting seriously. He had read something about it somewhere, or so he thought. He commended the dectective initiative that More had shown.

"When are you going to test Doull then?" he asked eagerly.

More remembered the pistol he had lost, which was now more than likely in Doull's possession.

"Soon," he replied, "soon."

The pistol was indeed in Magnus' hands. He had thought it a strikingly good bit of luck when he found it there in the toon below the house, and he kept it on his person at all times, while still developing his plans. It might prove useful to him yet.

There was revenge on his mind, and he had the courage of a man already believing himself doomed. He planned a trip or two into the lion's den, for he had things to say, to the policeman, to the minister and to the whole bloody lot of them. Them that had alerted the police to his return in the first place.

There was revenge on Magnus' mind all right.

And if they hanged him, then he hanged with the grace of a pure-hearted man, who had said all the secret things on his conscience, and told of the wrongs he observed. He might even begin a revolution, he grinned.

He thought of the words he had read in the *Art of the People* by William Morris.

> It is good for a man who thinks seriously, seriously to face his fellows, and speak out whatever really burns in him, so that men might seem less strange to one another, and misunderstanding, the fruitless cause of aimless strife may be avoided . . .

A profound effect that had on him, when he first read it, on a late night watch while the ship ploughed through the ocean. He had sat, and in his poor hand had written his own version of Morris' truth, his scrawl lit by the moon.

"Whit du feels in da heart, bring forth."

This he had folded and placed in his pocketbook. He was twenty-one then, full of ideals and full of a sense of maltreatment by Fate. Purity was his only concern.

What had happened to those fine ideals? Was it the

life at sea that had tainted them with rum and withered them in whores' beds? Whatever, he had lost those ideals, until that night in Bombay when young Jimmy Syme had his throat cut by the pimp pickpocket after his bankroll. That had sickened Magnus of the life. Jimmy was a fine young lad, not unlike Magnus himself at the same age, and Magnus knew that it could so easily have been himself that died in that sordid fashion. It was a wasted life, the boy not out of his teens.

That was what had spurred his return to Turmtillen. Although he had long thought of it, it was Jimmy Syme's tragic end that finally brought it to a crisis of decision.

The high hopes he had of his new life at Turmtillen! Like a fool, he'd believed that they would forget the past. Some had, but there were others like the minister and Robert Williamson that loved to dig the dirt. Well, Magnus was going to dig some of their dirt before he was through with Mirkwick, gallows or not.

They'd find him a trying enemy. He patted the pistol in his belt. He might even use it, if he had to. He might even set fire to the Haa House and watch as the fat old Morton burned in his bed. Whatever, there would be sparks flying soon in Mirkwick, that was for sure. Too many people were angry, too many hearts were soured.

Magnus fired with vengeance, and More with his pride hurt were but two of them. Not one soul in the parish rested easy that night. Perhaps it was a particular configuration of the heavenly bodies. Perhaps some time of tension in the earth's crust at Mirkwick. Everyone felt it. Aald Seemon swore he could taste it in the air.

The muskets were primed and ready for battle. It would not be long before the first shot was fired.

Chapter Sixteen

Gale Force

The wind switched round to the north-east that day. It grew stronger and stronger and the sky filled with ominous clouds, which opened in the afternoon with such a deluge that nobody cared to remain outdoors.

As was usual, the alehouse filled with idle men. Conversation grew louder and louder as the beer and spirits flowed.

Haakie Manson kept all ears open.

It was days like this when he learned most.

Wind drummed on the window with crazed fingertips, gusting rain into every dry cranny. The crofting men that still had crops in the field sat glaring into open space, visions of a struggle to salvage their harvest tormenting them.

A strange ship moored in the mouth of the voe. Attention focussed on it.

Haakie listened.

She looked a sleek vessel from what they could see, built for speed. Men who had sailed expressed their opinions as to possible origins. Voices surmised similarities with others they knew.

They watched as a boat was lowered over the side and set out for the pier.

The wind was now gusting gale force. The rowing boat pivoted on the waves, rolling bow to stern like a seesaw. Slowly the crew guided her to shore.

"A few extra customers da night, Haakie," someone observed.

"It's a pity Nina's gone, she coulda made her fortune da night."

Bubbling laughter spread through the tavern.

Five wet sailors entered the smoky atmosphere, shaking themselves like dogs.

They were foreign, probably Scandinavian.

Haakie had picked up a bit of Norwegian in his time as proprietor.

"Göddag," he began, but he was met with blank looks.

"Ruske?" he tried again, without success.

They muttered among themselves, and one of them, a tall nail-hard man with laughing eyes, pointed to a glass standing on the counter.

Haakie held up five fingers, and the stranger nodded.

The glasses filled, they took them and drank them down thirstily. Gold coins exchanged hands, and Haakie's eyes glistened with greed. If the storm kept up he might do a good night's business.

The glasses were filled again. The men took them and went to a corner seat, where they surrounded a table and sat muttering. Haakie strained to hear. He was suspicious, and didn't like the idea of not knowing who they were. It was a rare thing that he didn't and this made it all the worse.

The leader had a look about him. Those eyes were nefarious, Haakie decided, their humour concealed cunning.

Creepin' Ertie left the smithy on an errand for the blacksmith.

He wanted fish from Aald Seemon, who was ashore again, after the storm had driven him from his past-time around the rocks.

The cripple intercepted him as he walked home from the noost. Ertie explained his errand.

"He says he'll pay you when next he sees you."

Seemon shrugged indifferently.

"I've more fish dan I can use, tell him."

They stood in the shelter of a stone dyke. Out beyond Hulterness, in the sound between the mainland and the distant isle of Nissay where the trows and goblins of ages past were reputed to have lived, the waves were ten feet tall.

Seemon unhooked a half-a-dozen piltocks from the stick he carried them on.

He gave them to Ertie who put them in a bag he had bought.

"I see we have visitors in Mirkwick," said Seemon, stuffing his pipe, and indicating with its stem the ship now half-shrouded in a drizzly haze.

"Ertie," said Seemon suddenly, "Whit does du mind about Tammas Pole? I've been thinking lately a lot aboot it, since Magnus Doull came back and all, and I wis trying to mind if there wisna some rumour about Tammas at da time being involved in some smugglin' or idder, across in Scalloway."

Ertie seemed not to listen.

"Magnus Doull hurts people," he said, "He does not think of others."

The old fishermen lit his pipe. Ertie was behaving strangely. He was not the polite, friendly man he had been.

Seemon pulled his collar up, and took up his pole of fish.

"Weel, I'll be off noo, or Bessie'll be worryin'."

Ertie did not reply.

"Here," said Seemon, "Here's twa piltocks ta deesel."

But Ertie didn't hear him. He too set off into the gale carrying his bag of fish for the blacksmith. As he came into the shelter of the houses at the pier-head, he was met by five sailors at the gate to the factor's house.

They approached him.

''Hey, cripple!'' shouted one. ''Come here.''

Ertie stopped. His eyes skirted about him to see if he could escape, but with his leg it would not have been possible. He held onto his fish tightly.

The sailors surrounded him.

''We just want to ask a few questions,'' asked a smiling faced one.

Ertie stared blankly.

''Where can we find Thomas Sutherland? Come on, we won't hurt you.''

Ertie said nothing. He sensed something about these men that told him they were not good.

''Ach, it's no use, he's mute.'' said another one.

The first stepped forward.

''Mute, eh? We'll see about that.''

And he delivered a powerful winding punch to the cripple's gut. Ertie doubled up, dropping his fish, the shock of the blow causing him to cry out.

He felt someone take hold of his hair, and the hand hauled tight till it seemed he would lose his scalp.

''Where's Thomas Sutherland?'' the man repeated.

Ertie mumbled something incoherent, and felt his hair yanked tight again.

''I don't know,'' he stammered, ''He's been away.''

''But he's back now isn't he? And he owes us money. A lot of money. And if you don't help us get it, we're going to kill you.''

Ertie kept his teeth gritted, trying to resist the pain.

''Kill me then.''

A sharp stab of needle pain between his shoulders. Ertie fell to the ground, his face contorted.

One of the seamen swung his boot. It caught the

cripple on the side of his head. Colours faded into unconsciousness, wild dreams of formless confusion blanked his brain.

The sailors disappeared into the shadows again. Ertie lay there motionless on the cobbles as the rain pelted down on his mishapen body. At his feet, the bag of fish splayed open over the paving.

And at the window of the little house above the store, the eyes of Isabella watched, terrified.

Chapter Seventeen

Words used as Weapons

The bell tolled, slow and tuneless, the same brass note repeated over and over. The figures could be seen converging on the kirk from all directions, little groups of them, meeting, massing into larger, like tributaries into the mainstream.

Sunday best. Clothes smelling of mothballs. One suit for a lifetime, carefully preserved, used one day out of seven, and at funerals and weddings and the like.

Black sombre figures. Whole families, striding out towards the kirk, meeting neighbour families, and travelling with them, until outside the kirk itself, a crowd gathered, filtering slowly through the small door, into the ice cold atmosphere of presbyterian worship.

A plain protestant kirk was the Mirkwick one. Three windows on either side, without decoration, plain glass; wooden benches down the length of the kirk, with a central aisle leading to the pulpit, hanging precipitously over the pews. From this point of superiority, the minister would give vent to religious spoutings.

The people took their seats, solemn faced. The great bell continued to toll. More and more packed into the kirk, till the seats were full bar one. This was the laird's seat, and was kept separate from the rest of the kirk by wooden barriers. It ran at right angles to the rest of the pews, against the western wall.

When all the rest of the congregation had taken their seats, the party from the Haa entered. The Lady Isobella first, followed by her son, then Ellen Mitchell, and then the factor.

The kirk elders were about to close the door, the signal for the Reverend Cunningham to emerge from the vestry, when a foot stopped the door.

Voices whispered angrily at the porch, and the congregation turned slyly to see the cause of the commotion.

Voices whispered.

"It's him.

"I saa his red hair."

Word sped through the pews like the plague; Magnus Doull had come to the kirk!

Peter Jacobesen, the kirk elder, held the door firm against Magnus, his undertaker's face lit up with a red passion.

"Du's no' a member o' dis congregation," he drilled through clenched teeth, intending this to be quiet, but the whole parish heard him.

"And wid du deny me da chance to repent?" came Magnus' reply, mocking.

Lady Isobelle leant over and whispered something to the factor, who looked at her twice before he rose and went to the door. He in turn whispered in the ear of Peter Jacobesen, and the kirk elder let go of his grip of the door.

It swung full open, and there indeed was Magnus Doull. What had been a suspicion was confirmed. The hubbub increased.

Doull stood there in the doorway for a few seconds. His eyes moved slowly about the congregation. He saw faces he knew, worried, staring at him as if he were the Devil himself. He supped in the atmosphere.

"Take a seat, dan," snapped Jacobesen angrily.

Magnus entered the kirk, and pushed into the first

empty seat. It was Jacobesen's own, reserved for him when he had closed the door on the assembly! The elder girned at him, and the self-righteous Margaret, his wife, looked away from Magnus as far as she could crane her neck. He sat next to her! The murderer himself.

Balance was restored, the door was shut, and Jacobesen was forced to sit by it on an old wooden chair from the porch.

Mary Williamson, the organist, began to play, squeaky breathy notes. The vestry door opened, and the Reverend Cunningham appeared in his long flowing robes, black with a fringe of white about his neck. He entered the pulpit and placed the books he carried on the lectern.

The congregation which had risen when he entered sat down again. Except one. Magnus. He sat there, a sore thumb, in his working britches and sweat soiled shirt, red hair ablaze.

Cunningham saw him. A look of surprise and displeasure passed across his face.

"We will sing Hymn number 149," he said and the organ began to play. It squeaked out two exemplary stanzas of melody, and the congregation rose again.

Cunningham took little part in the singing. Doull had not risen. He merely sat there staring straight at the minister's face, his gaze unshifting, unblinking. It was the most blatant snub of the church's sanctity. Cunningham grew angrier and angrier as the hymn progressed, feeling himself and all he believed in challenged, quite openly in the one place where he was the master. Being in the kirk his courage was greater, for the two hundred souls seated on the pews in front of him were his army.

The hymn had seven verses, each following the droning melodic shape of the first. Magnus eyes never left the minister's face, and all the while the religious zeal of the Reverend Cunningham transformed into personal mallice towards this transgressor.

In the pulpit, he was king. Even the laird looked up to him with modest face. How dare this murderer come here, to God's place and challenge the minister, God's emmissary, with his lawless eyes.

He would see him hang, if not for the murder, then for this sacriligeous behaviour.

The hymn finished and the congregation settled, coughing modestly, into the wooden pews.

The Reverend Cunningham opened the Bible at a pre-set place, and began to speak, but he did not refer to his notes, rather to the anger inside him.

"'Good people of this parish, we have gathered together here today to give thanks to the Lord God Almighty. To offer up to Him our souls, in order that He may cleanse them, and send us out once more into our daily lives purified and at peace within ourselves.

"'Sin is a part of our daily lives. Not one day passes that evil thoughts do not pierce the fortress of our convictions. Yet these are normally small transgressions that we come to ask forgiveness for. Sins which can be purged from our hearts by the reaffirmation of our faith. Yet none the less, these are sins that can lead to hell and damnation, should they remain unconfessed. Remain unconfessed, and the flames of the fires of Purgatory will consume your souls in the Eternal. There is no fact plainer than that.

"'I ask you then to consider the weight that lies upon the soul of a man who has committed a major sin. For example, examine the soul of a murderer, a man who has broken that most plain of the Commandments, 'Thou shalt not kill . . .' Is he not damned already, while still alive in this world of Men, consumed with the flames of

Hell? Does the very brimstone not reek from his nostrils, from his clothes?

"Consider, good parishioners, consider . . .

"There is one among us who has a heavy weight on his conscience. A man who has blatantly defied the sanctity of this, the House of the Lord God Almighty, who has come here with evil in his heart. I speak of one Magnus Doull, of Turmtillen. He is here today, among us, tainted with the smell of brimstone, his soul the possession of the very Devil himself . . .

"Stand up, Magnus Doull, I command it in the name of the Lord . . ."

The minister's voice echoed through the kirk. Heads swivelled on shoulders. Margaret Jacobesen seated next the 'murderer' swooned, fell to her knees. Brimstone, horrible sulphurous odours seemed to pervade her senses.

"Lord God protect me, she sobbed, "I smell it, I smell da brimstone."

"Stand up, Magnus Doull . . . the minister commanded again.

Magnus leant over to the hysterical Mrs Jacobesen.

"Brimstone be buggered. I wis in da byre afore I came here . . ."

And then he stood up.

"Yes, Reverend Minister, it's me, da Devil's ain, Magnus Doull."

The Reverend Cunningham became hysterical himself, his voice quivering as he appealed to the congregation . . .

"See . . . See how he admits it? O Lord God that is in Heaven, protect us, smite down thine enemy."

Others joined Margaret Jacobesen on their knees overcome. Others trembled, awaiting the inevitable thunderbolt.

"I defy thee, God of these hypocrites, I defy thee in thy own house," cried Magnus, waving his arms above his head, his hair like the flames of Hell itself.

"Smite me down, O Impotent One, show yoursel'."

The whole kirk trembled on the brink of obliteration. Seconds, longer than centuries ticked past, slow unbearably slow.

The minister began to pray.

"Our Father that is in Heaven . . ."

The voices joined him, one by one, until the whole congregation, shaken by tumultuous fear, prayed together.

Only one voice failed to join them. It was Ellen Mitchell's. She watched, her body frozen, this scene of supernatural tensions, unable to move even her mouth. She seemed to slip into another dimension. Suddenly everything about her was silent and she felt herself being transported out of her body until she reached the rafters of the kirk. Colours faded together, forms lost all meaning. Only the Spirit mattered. From this vantage point of self release, she watched the praying congregation, and saw the cloud that hid their souls. She saw her own body motionless in the laird's pew, saw her mistress and her son and the factor stock still, timeless, shaken by fear out of their consciousness.

And she saw Magnus Doull, still standing, disbelieving, watching the praying crowd. She reached inside him, opened his soul, and found it clean!

And with that she sank back inside herself again. The pain of re-entering her body stung her and she fainted.

The thunderbolt did not come.

And the congregation heard a voice begin to speak, a voice of trembling intensity. It was Magnus. They listened, still praying, fearful.

"You call this da House o' da Lord. Pah! It is da House o' Oppression. A tool of da ruling classes to keep da poor fae rebelling. Dey tell you of Hell-Fire and Damnation. Dey tell you you will be burned in the Eternal if you do not do as dey instruct. Poor fools dat you are, can't you see? It's your own ignorance dey exploit. Dis man dat caa's himsel' God's representative, whit proof does he have o' dat? The Kirk is a parasite living aff your labours. Cast it aff, reject it, claim your freedom. God will not strike you doon, any more dan he has me. Are you sheep to be led wherever dey tell you, even if it is to da slaughter? I can't believe it. I can't believe dat dere's no even wan o' you capable of free thought.''

The prayers continued, went on over and over, led by the Reverend Cunningham.

Magnus looked at them all with their heads bent to the floor and their mouths opening automatically.

He felt a bad taste at the back of his mouth, and he spat, then turned and flung open the doors of the kirk.

''Here,'' he shouted, ''Here is God, here in dis wind.''

And with that he was gone.

The gale swept through the open door, raising dust and blowing cobwebs from the rafters. The congregation continued to pray, with their heads lowered. Mother's hands held their children tight, and enforced their silence. A sobbing began from the mouth of Margaret Jacobesen, to be echoed by many others.

The minister at last stood up in the pulpit once again. He was white, his face like the sheet of a shroud.

''Father of us all,'' he spoke softly, ''we place our trust in Thee. We know that this sinner will be justly punished. Oh God, protect us. Purify us, and let not these evil words lead any of thy flock astray.''

And on and on he went in his droning voice, till the calm was restored as far as it could be. Then Mary Williamson began to pump the organ . . .

The twenty-third Psalm.

In full discordant voice, the people sang as one. All except Ellen. She regained consciousness in the midst of the minister's prayers, raised her head and scanned the kirk. It was a dream. It had to be. She had never seen the like of it, had never heard words so powerful, used not as a ritual, but as a weapon.

She laid her head on the hymnbook in front of her, confused and saddened by it all. A hand caressed her hair. It was the Lady Morton's. She looked into her mistress' eyes and saw the same sadness, and the same confusion. For them, religion and Christianity were far removed from the scene in the kirk today. It would trouble them greatly, these evil happenings in the Lord's place. But the burden would not be one of fear or anger, as it would for the majority of people here, but of regret.

Chapter Eighteen

Consequences

Magnus Doull was damned. He would burn in hell. Aa'body agreed on that. When More heard of the happenings at the kirk, he was delighted. Doull's actions had turned the whole parish against him, and that would make the policeman's plans much easier to implement.

The Reverend Cunningham was on the point of distraction following his ordeal in church. He had managed it fairly well, he thought, but it was a confrontation he could have done without. Doull's revolutionary outburst could only unsettle people, and with the drift of emigrants dissatisfied with their lot towards the colonies, Mirkwick was unstable, like many other places.

The minister was one of the few folk who knew anything of the social unrest on the mainland, in the big cities, where the poor folk were being stirred by groups of intellectuals under the banner of a new political standpoint — Socialism. He didn't know that Doull was familiar with these opinions, or that he had read a little of the works of the movement's leaders. He didn't even believe Magnus capable of reading.

Yet there was real danger in the person of the murder suspect, not merely to the hearts of the poor folk, but to the established system of rule. To the Kirk and to the Laird.

Things must be handled carefully. The sooner

Magnus Doull was silenced the better. There would be some among the parishioners whose heads were turned by his words, and it was conceivable that they would join him in time if he continued his present course.

The Kirk Elders supported the minister's vibrant suggestion in the vestry after the service, that no time should be wasted in capturing the fugitive. Regardless of his punishment in the next world, he would have first to face the consequences of his deeds in this. Peter Jacobsen, still fuming over the incident at the Kirk door, stated that the man was evil. They all agreed on this, all except Seemon, who kept quiet.

"But still we have no conclusive evidence," Cunningham clicked his tongue, and paused there in mid-sentence. They all looked at each other.

Hatred was running so feverishly through them, that this technicality seemed less important than before. It was a proper army that was massing to see the hanging.

"I remember him," said Ellen.

The Lady Isobelle looked at her in surprise.

"Who?" she asked.

"Why, the man at the church this morning," replied Ellen. She had been trying to place the face in memory all morning.

"He was on the same ship as I when I first arrived here. I knew I'd seen him before."

The Lady Isobelle stood up and walked over to the huge fireplace. She warmed herself, thoughtfully clicking a set of beads in her palms.

"Do you think there was any truth in what he said, this Magnus Doull?" she asked after a period of thought.

Ellen looked out across the windy plain of Mirkwick, through the second floor window. High up on Crugness, she saw the tiny dwelling of Turmtillen, tucked in the headland's bosom.

"I don't know. I suppose it is a poor way of life. I

suppose they must have hardships. But whether one can blame the Church for those or not, I don't know. I feel very ignorant of the way the people live here. I've been here almost seven months now, and I've never seen anything of the place really, except through the windows. I never thought of it like that before, but it is true."

She turned her attention back to Lady Morton.

Her Ladyship smiled.

"Then I must be many times more ignorant, Ellen, for I've been here much longer, and I know as little as you."

She left the fireplace and settled in a comfortable sofa.

"I've never thought of them as people before. It's very remiss of one, I know. All these years, I've lived the greater part of my life believing that it was matters of the spirit that I care for. Now I realise that people are important as well. What a change in all of us since you arrived, my dear."

Her thoughts went to her husband, who was a very different person since Ellen's youthful purity touched him.

"I can't help thinking that there will come a day when you will leave us.

It's selfish, I know, but you've brought so much life to this house. I can't help wondering what will become of us."

Ellen lowered her head.

"No, ma'am, it's more complex than that. I am only the instrument of the Lord."

"Yes, my dear, but it is you that he has chosen for his work here, and it is you that personifies his magnaminity."

The housemaid brought them a tray of afternoon tea. She placed it on a small table by the sofa's side, curtseyed, and left.

"Thank you, my dear," said Lady Morton, as Ellen poured and passed her a cup.

"It was sinful of that man all the same, to enter the House of God in the way that he did. No once can deny that, regardless of the rights and wrongs of his arguments and the strength of his feeling."

"I know," said Ellen. She was musing over the strange experience that had befallen her at church that morning, trying to find the right words to explain it all to her mistress. She desperately wanted to share it.

"I believe he has been terribly wronged," she said at last.

"Wronged?" Lady Isobelle replied in surprise, "But my dear, I thought he was a murderer?"

Ellen sipped her tea.

"Yes, well, I don't know the truth of that." She seemed to lose her courage.

"It's just that . . . "

"Go on . . . " her mistress encouraged.

"I had the weirdest experience in the Church this morning," she began, uncertain. "I seemed to be floating through the air, watching myself and all the people sitting there . . . does that seem ridiculous to you?"

"Not at all. I've heard of that phenomenon before," she answered. "The flight of the spirit out of the physical body in times of stress."

Ellen wasn't listening.

"It's because of this that I believe Magnus Doull has been wronged. It's very difficult to explain, but I had the feeling that I could see his soul, and that it was pure like a saint's. Without a stain."

Lady Morton put down her cup and saucer, and rose from her seat. Her distant attitude became suddenly intense and serious. Ellen watched her pace the room and felt the turmoil churning within.

All the while the beads clicked in her palm.

"When you say you saw into his soul, how did this feel?"

"I can't explain it. It wasn't me that saw, or rather it wasn't the me that sat alongside you. It was the me that was freed from my body, floating through the atmosphere, like a ghost. And then I just knew."

She ran out of words.

"I can't explain . . . "

Lady Isobelle came and sat beside her.

My dear, have you ever felt this power before. Tell me truly now."

Ellen shook her head.

"Not like that. But once when I was eleven, I foresaw my grandfather's death. It was awful. I felt as if I had killed him."

Her eyes filled with tears.

Lady Morton took her hand.

"Oh Ellen, if you have had a vision, and this man is innocent, then we are implicated by the fact of our knowledge. Oh Ellen," she spoke softly.

Her hands caressed the girls hair.

"Your gifts are not so easy to bear, I see. And I that thought your life so simple and straightforward. But you have your burden like all creatures of the flesh."

Together they sat, holding tight to their love, both aware of the presence of a force that neither of them could control.

Ellen whimpered a little, so sensitive was she to the gravity of the moment.

What could they do? They were women, allowed so little say in the affairs of the estate.

"They will hang him. No one does what he has done and goes unpunished. Poor misguided man, if only there was something we could do."

"Ellen, there is something we can do. We can pray from our hearts for his soul. The Lord will listen, and will be merciful."

At that moment the door opened, and the laird entered, puffing and panting.

"Good afternoon, my dears," he breezed, You seem extremely cosy."

Lady Isobelle made a signal with her eyes.

"Ellen? What's the matter?" the laird asked, sincerely concerned.

"Leave us, please," said his wife sharply.

He was shocked by her tone, and did as she requested.

He had still not heard of the scene at the Kirk that morning, but as he descended the staircase, he saw Sutherland the factor, waiting for him.

"Afternoon, Sutherland," he said, his good spirits swept away by his wife's brusqueness. They entered the library.

Sutherland told the laird of the morning's happenings, and how Doull had escaped before he could be stopped. The laird listened, finding the whole story fantastic, gaping with incredulity.

"To think that I missed it all," he bellowed cheerfully, "What on earth prevented me from attending today of all days? Why this is turning out to be the best entertainment we've had for years!"

"I'm afraid, sir, that this isn't light-hearted nonsense. Doull said some strong things today, words that to me smacked of an uprising."

The laird poured himself and the factor a glass of brandy.

"Surely not in Mirkwick? These people are about as rebellious as monks," he said, laughing at his own joke.

"Sir, I beg you take this seriously. If you had only been present, you would have seen for yourself. This man will have to be apprehended before he goes any further. The equilibrium of the whole community is at stake."

"Well what about this policeman or detective, or

whatever? Hasn't he done anything about it? He must have been here months by now.''

Sutherland shrugged.

''They have no evidence against Doull.''

''Yes, I see,'' he said, but he didn't. ''What do you propose we do about it?''

Sutherland's eyes narrowed. He took a sip of brandy, and set his glass upon the table.

''It will cost money,'' he warned.

''How much?'' he asked.

''A lot. I'll have to bribe the policeman,'' said Sutherland, averting his eyes from the Laird's, awaiting his reaction.

''I see,'' he mused. ''And you think this is necessary?''

''I do, sir, in fact it is absolutely vital.''

The laird gave his consent.

''So what's to be done then?'' he asked.

The lips of the factor moved imperceptibly.

''We'll hang him . . . ''

Chapter Nineteen

The Robbery

Robert Williamson went into the office on Monday morning as usual at eight-thirty.

The sight that met his eyes struck him dumb.

The old cast iron safe where he kept his takings, and most of his savings forbye, was empty, the door swinging open casually, the rape complete. He saw the broken window where the thief had gained entry.

Had he forgotten to lock the safe?

He couldn't remember. It was all so much of a habit.

Desperately he tried to recall the contents of the safe. There had been six days takings from the shop, some of his own money besides, and cash belonging to the Post Office.

Wind breezed through the broken window. The shopkeeper took an old coat and tried to stuff it into the gap. His hand slipped, and piece of glass still sticking in the window frame slit his finger. The blood oozed out.

"Oh God," he cried, and ran out of the office, just as Peter Jacobsen appeared.

"Whit's wrong?" the boy asked, concerned.

"They've cleaned the safe . . . and now I've cut mysel."

Peter leapt over the counter, and looked into the office.

For some reason, he smiled.

"Peter, Peter, have we anything I can put on this

damned cut, will you look, please?'' squealed the merchant.

He was running about like a chicken with its head cut off, the blood seeping through his fingers, dripping all over the floor.

The lad took him into the office and made him sit down. Then he ran to the house next door and fetched the family.

More the policeman followed behind, still wearing the napkin tucked under his chin from the breakfast table.

Mrs Williamson, like a high-pitched Florence Nightingale, ran to her husband's side. The two daughters turned away from the sight of the blood.

''Robert . . . Robert,'' whimpered his wife, tying an old towel about his hand to catch the blood.

''They've cleaned the safe out,'' repeated the shopkeeper dimly. He felt faint at the red of his own blood.

''Here, Peter, help him through to the house,'' said his wife.

Mary the elder daughter went to the door.

''I'll fetch Bessie,'' she said.

''Good girl,'' said her father with a weak smile.

More was left alone in the shop with Agnes. He went into the office as if he owned the place, and began inspecting the safe.

''No signs of it being forced. Mind you, it doesn't look as if it would take much forcing,'' he sneered.

''And if the thief really knew his business, a skeleton key would not be hard to come by,'' he said re-emerging from the office.

He caught sight of the slim figure of Agnes Williamson slumping to the floor, and vaulted the counter with surprising agility. He picked her head from the floor.

''Come, my dear, it's only a little blood. Always looks worse than it really is.''

She opened her eyes slightly.

"It's not that, she said. "I know who did it."

The scandal of the robbery over-shadowed even Magnus Doull's appearance at the kirk the previous day. Of course, nobody had any doubts as to who had done it. As Agnes told them later, the five sailors from the mysterious ship had hung around the pierhead all Saturday night, and had plenty of time to make their getaway before the shop reopened on Monday morning.

More sent a telegram to the police in Lerwick explaining that he would take charge of the crime, as he was on the scene, but there was little to be done about it all now. The robbers had escaped with their loot.

When Isabella emerged weeping, telling of the sight she had seen, when the men had assaulted poor Ertie, all was confirmed, and everyone began searching for the cripple. He was nowhere to be seen. People surmised that he must have surprised the criminals at their dirty work, and paid the penalty.

Williamson had lost more than he could afford to. And as there was no proof of the safe having been forced, and the idea of the sailors having a skeleton key seeming preposterous, he must have, as he had feared, left it unlocked.

The Post Office would take a poor view of that.

It was late afternoon when Creepin' Ertie finally appeared. He was able to confirm Isabella's garbled story of the assault, and had the bruises to prove it. He said they had dumped him for dead in one of the store's no longer used at the pier. That he had risen out of a tangle of nets and ropes of aged rotting equipment, not knowing what had happened to him.

A crowd gathered about him. He was a hero. Folk pestered him with questions. Seemon watched from the alehouse door. He smiled. The old cripple was glorying in it all.

"And did you come upon them at their crime?" asked More.

The cripple hesitated.

"Crime?"

"The robbery at the shop," the policeman coached.

Ertie frowned. At the shop? No, surely it was outside the factor's house. He looked at Isabella, but she was no help, muttering away to herself.

Suddenly a hand shoved a tobacco pouch in the cripple's face.

"Of course he did, the brave fellow that he is," said a voice.

Ertie looked around, in surprise.

It was the factor.

He had an odd look in his eye as he offered Ertie a smoke for his pipe. Ertie refused, trying to decipher the factor's meaning.

Was this a secret he must keep? He was good at secrets.

At Turmtillen, Meenie watched Magnus grow more and more agitated. He sat by the window all Sunday and all day Monday muttering to himself, as if rehearsing a speech. Yet all the while a silence loomed large and ominous over him. He seemed to believe that it was only a matter of time until they came for him.

Meenie spread the cards that day, looking desperately for some clue, but the patterns were abstracted. She did not possess the insight with which to formulate a picture of the future. The Death Card appeared again in the Sixth place, and the Fool in the Tenth.

Was it Magnus? Was he the fool, the victim of his own folly?

She carried on her life as she always did that day, attending to the routine. It was the only thing she could do. Changes went on around her, but Meenie had already left the shifting sands of material existence. Her days were timeless, measured only by the rhythm of day and night.

When she met Bessie Sinclair at the dykes of Shalderwick, on her way home from seeing to the injury Robert Williamson had sustained, and heard of the robbery and the attack on Creepin' Ertie, it only confirmed in her mind the sense of traumatic change.

None appeared free of its influence.

The skin of life in Mirkwick was becoming afflicted with sores which would spread and infect the whole body before they began to heal. And when they healed, the scars would be there for a long long time.

Meenie didn't care to be around then. It was for Magnus that her heart ached. He seemed to be at the centre of all the swirling mists misdirecting and disorientating, yet he had come to Turmtillen with such good intentions and worked so hard on the croft.

Monday was a dark day in the croft of the Doull's.

Magnus mumbled to himself, growing angry when he tripped up verbally. Meenie moped about. She couldn't find the word to get through to him. When she tried he looked at her blankly, his eyes reflecting the fact that she could no longer see inside him . . .

Chapter Twenty

Good Parishioners Once More

The good parishioners assembled in the manse on Monday night, the cast the same as before.

"Now is the time for action," the Reverend Cunningham began, before the folk had time to take their seats.

"This man is a danger to the very foundations of our community. He is a viper loose among us. Had we any doubts before, the episode at the Church yesterday will have rubbed them from our minds. His behaviour scorned everything that we believe in. And he must be punished."

Seemon nodded his head.

"Aye, it was a terrible thing Magnus did. He soiled wir kirk with his words."

Robert Williamson tweeked the corner of his moustache.

"Yes, he must pay allright."

"Then we're all agreed," Cunningham queried, and the heads all nodded.

A silence descended on the room. The parishioners waited for the minister to continue.

"We have a plan, that is to say, the special constable and myself. Now I think we've all heard of the box that

Mr More has brought with him to Mirkwick, but in case anyone hasn't, let me enlarge on it's uses. The technique is called 'Fingerprinting'. It's relatively new, but it has been used in India, where it was developed. I consider More to have shown considerable initiative in obtaining this piece of equipment, and I intend to commend him to his superiors after this case is closed. Mr More, if you'd like to come in now,'' he said opening the library door.

The little constable came into the room.

''Now you've all met this gentleman before, I'm sure, but . . . ''

The minister was interrupted by Seemon.

''Just a minute, minister, are you saying dat dis fingerprinting business is serious? I was under da impression, as were a lot o' ither folk, dat dis wis a ploy to panic Magnus into given hisel' awa'.''

''I don't understand you. You mean you thought that Mr More was trying to deceive you?''

The policeman protested at this.

''Well, it aa' sounded so unlikely, signatures on da ends of fingers, and all,'' Seemon defended himself.

''We aa' assumed it wis a trick''.

More said angrily that it was no trick, but pure science, and that he should have realised by now how backward the people of Mirkwick were.

''Now Mr More, it's a misunderstanding, nothing else. It happens to the best of us,'' said the minister, trying to calm things, as the policeman and Aald Seemon glared at each other.

Mrs Williamson, sweet as a sugar lump, smiled at the detective.

''I'm sure Mr More would never do anything to deceive us, would you?''

This caused him to forget his pique, and give the lady an awkward grin.

An uneasy silence.

Then the minister began again.

"Well, to the plan," he said. "We will need the help of some of you. Haakie and Seemon, you two have had more to say to Doull than any of the rest of us since his return — I am not criticising — in fact it is that fact, and that alone which can help make our plan succeed. We have, you see, to make him trust us, so that we can obtain a print of his fingers. You, Seemon, must entice him to have a drink with you in the tavern, and you Haakie, must keep his glass for the constable to use in his experiment. Then he will be able to match those with those on the all important bottle. If they are the same, and after yesterday I am in doubt they will be, then we have him."

All listened closely.

Seemon spoke.

"Why doesn't he just go and get his fingerprints?" he asked, pointing at More. "Why do we have to go to all dis trouble?"

"Because I have good reason to suspect that Doull is armed and that he will use this weapon without hesitation. It's good sense to take as few risks as possible," the policeman leered.

This was agreed by all except Seemon and Haakie.

"It's his job to take risks, not mine nor Haakie's," he protested.

"But can't you see, for you there are no risks?" Cunningham encouraged.

"I don't like it," said Seemon. "It's devious."

Haakie, who had been unusually quiet, joined the discussion.

"And whit if it's not his fingerprints? Then he'll ken it wis me and Seemon dat trapped him, won't he?"

The minister smiled.

"Surely there is no question of his innocence after yesterday's performance?" he asked. "Seemon, you yourself said he would have to be punished not so long ago."

"I said whit he did in da kirk wis wrong. Dat wis all."

Robert Williamson asked if Seemon was scared.

"Robert, du should ken better." It was all Seemon had to say. Anyone who knew the tales of his exploits at sea should have known not to question the old man's bravery.

Tea and cakes were distributed by Mrs Williamson. Isabella was not well enough after Ertie's beating, so she stood in as hostess.

This was not really women's business. They were here to discuss a hanging, and so Mrs Williamson suggested that the men go into the library to continue their discussion.

"Much as I want to see him brought to justice, it's not really the kind of talk for ladies, is it?" she said.

And so the men went into the library, the minister leading the way.

"It's a question of morality, really," he said to Seemon, aside from the rest. "You are in a position to do the whole community a service by bringing this whole nasty business to a close. I can't put it plainer than that."

Seemon Sinclair lit his pipe now that he was in men's quarters, and puffed on it.

"Yea, I suppose du's right, minister. Though I still don't like it."

Nor did Haakie. He was strangely subdued that night, sucking on his lip thoughtfully. He listened as they approached the subject of the capture of Magnus Doull, to More as he described from his catalogue of criminal experience just how to behave in the presence of a murderer.

"You must forget that he is a killer. Forget your hatred of him. Treat him as you would anyone else. If at all tense in his company, he will sense it and bolt. For when under stress, as he must be at this moment, a man's senses become sharper. The psychological approach. That's the way to do it."

The minister confirmed this.

"Are you listening, Haakie?" he asked, annoyed at Haakie's silence.

"Yes, yes, I am," said Haakie.

"Is there anything you're not sure of? Any questions you want to ask?" said More.

"No," said Haakie, "I ken exactly whit you're doing."

They all looked at him, Seemon too, as if he were on a different wavelength. For the last phrase had not been said with good grace.

But Haakie would say no more. He listened to the rest of them as they went over and over the 'plan', making sure there would be no mistakes.

"Well, gentlemen," said Cunningham, handing out glasses of port wine, "Here's to success."

And they raised their glasses to the shadow of Magnus Doull swinging from the gallows.

Chapter Twenty-One

The Snare

There was no need to hunt out Magnus. He had no intention of hiding any longer. In his heart he desired only to see the business ended, to put the finishing touches to his own downfall and have done with it.

On Tuesday morning, as the crowd assembled waiting for the steamer to appear, Magnus set out from Turmtillen. Meenie watched him go. Her old eyes filled with tears.

The sun fought clouds for supremacy in a mottled sky, patches of light blotching the land in alternate moving patterns. Wind high above chased the clouds to foreign places.

Magnus filled his lungs with brisk air. He had half expected to be visited by the forces of law after his outburst in the kirk, but here he was being given another chance to voice his opinions. It was an opportunity he would not waste.

The steamer arrived on time. A flag fluttered from the mast in honour of the captain's daughter, who was on board celebrating her twenty-first birthday. This unexpected gaiety formed on a topic for discussion among the waiting crowd.

Magnus came into the crowd as the flit-boat returned to the pier. Aald Seemon saw him coming, and elbowed Haakie.

"See's du. Dere he is."

Haakie peered through the crowd. There indeed was the red-haired figure basking in his infamy, as heads turned to look at him. People drew back, remembering the minister's damning words on Sunday.

"Good-day to you aa'. Man, it's fine to see you aa'," grinned Magnus, his red hair flaming.

Eyes watched him but no mouths moved. The men in their beards and caps stood in front of their woman-folk, subsconsciously protecting them.

"You're a fine body a' folk, men, women and bairns alike. Fine upstanding folk dat canna wait to see me hang. Evil Magnus Doull, aye, dat's me. Well, maybe hanging's da best thing for folk like me, for I'll never fit into your idea of whit life should be like. You just take whit's given you by dem that dole it out. You never question it. You never ask why things should be da way dey are. You just hand it all over to dem, aa'thing you work so hard for during da year. Well, I canna live in a world like dat, so maybe if you hang me you'll be doing me a favour. Dan you can aa' go on, year after year, in your slavery, quite happy as lang as dere's nane like me to point out your errors or da wrongs done to you. But you'll no' hang me till I've telt you, till I've rid my self of aa' da sorrows dat I see."

His tongue spoke rapidly, slipping round the words with an eloquence that surprised even himself.

A voice from the crowd called . . .

"Sorrows? Na, Magnus, du's da only sorrow round here."

A few people laughed, but the most were disturbed by the hate in Magnus' voice.

"Aye, sorrows, sorrows of wasted lives, lived in the middle o' petty jealousy and mistrust. Dat's da sorrows I speak of, though you widna see dem, living in da midst o' dem."

The flit-boat discharged its cargo onto the pier, and Robert Williamson came out to collect the mailsacks.

Magnus focussed on the shopkeeper.

"Noo dere's a man wha's conscience you should examine. Da shopkeeper himsel'."

But no one was listening.

Behind Magnus' back, two men walked briskly to the alehouse door and talked to Haakie and Seemon. It was the minister and the Special Constable More.

"Look at him, and da life dat he leads, and ask whit it is dat gives him dat right to live off your labours."

No one heard him. Seemon moved forward through the crowd which parted before him.

He stood before the revolutionary, pipe in hand.

"Dat's powerful words, Magnus. Most rebellious I would say."

Magnus looked at him, his train of thought disturbed. His head was full of fire and a fever burned deep in his brow.

"Seemon," he said, recognising the old man through the mist of his delusion.

"Aye, Magnus, it's me, lad. Dis is an awful oncerry du's creating."

Magnus frowned. There was something about the old man's calm that disturbed him. It was not so long ago since Magnus had felt something akin to it himself. What had happened to make him forget his resolutions to live down his past? He struggled to remember. He was tired of trouble-making. What was he doing here?

"Man du's no weel," said Seemon, "Come in ada pub, and I'll buy dee a dram to set dee right."

Magnus scratched his head, causing the bristle hair to stand even more wildly on his head.

People waited silently to see the result.

"I . . . I canna . . . ," Magnus began. He quite suddenly forgot why he had come here.

"Man, du's no weel," Seemon repeated, and he meant it. He was quite concerned about the state of the red-haired man. Magnus seemed ready to collapse.

Seemon moved forward. Magnus clenched his fists, like a trapped and wounded animal preparing to defend itself.

The people drew back, not knowing what to expect.

"Come noo, Magnus lad, du needna fecht me."

Fists fell into loose nervous hands. He stepped forward and Seemon stood cautiously firm, his old lined face bearing a kindly smile. Magnus' eyes were scrutinising him, searching for some evidence of the old man's intentions.

Then his mood changed, quite abruptly.

"I'll tak' a dram wi' dee, Seemon, for auld times sakes."

He looked around him at the crowd who were watching every movement. They huddled closer under his stare, as if seeking security in numbers as the old proverb says.

Seemon and Magnus walked to the alehouse together, Magnus in front. The throng stood back, as one.

The minister and More were gone. Haakie moved out of the doorway to allow entry.

"Good day, Magnus," he said, "A revolution da day I see."

Seemon signalled to him to be quiet.

"Twa rums, Haakie," he said, "Magnus here is no feelin up ta da mark."

Haakie went behind the counter and poured the glasses. He had one himself. Magnus was trying to order the thoughts spinning in his head. Everything seemed foggy, and here in the poky tavern with its one window, the atmosphere confused him still more.

He took the rum and drank it down. He placed the empty glass on the counter, and the hand of Haakie Manson reached out unnoticed, to slip it under the bar.

It was done. Now all doubt could be eliminated.

The spirit idled down Magnus' gullet. It warmed him, seemed to aid the lucidity of his thought.

He sat down in the same seat that had accommodated him on his return to Mirkwick in the early summer. He thought of distant things, could not control the images appearing in his mind any longer.

"Revolution," he laughed cynically.

Seemon sat down too. There was no threat from the wild red hair now. He seemed very tame.

Magnus spoke again.

"Dere's a conspiracy against me."

Haakie and Seemon looked at each other.

"A conspiracy of all da Fates against me. Mind I said, Haakie when I came back here, dat day in da summer, I said I'd had enough of fights. Well look at me noo," he said, laughing bitterly, a laugh without humour.

Haakie set up another round of rum.

"Dat day, when I woke up, I had da worst headache I've ever had. I'd slept in a byre at Shalderwick. When I woke up, I needed a drink. I started out towards da Böd, and as I got to da pierhead, aa'body crowded aboot me. I was a murderer."

Seemon and Haakie listened without a word. Magnus was gazing into space, his mind far away.

"And noo dere's nothing to be done. Dere's nothing. Folk hang murderers." He sipped his rum, languidly.

"Revolution! You ken I do believe whit I say. I do believe dat dere's wrongs here in Mirkwick done to da poor folk. I'll no go back on my beliefs."

Seemon puffed on his pipe.

"I dare say dere's some truth in whit du says, but du can't just attack everything dat we folk believe in. We need wir beliefs same as dee. Maybe dere will be a better world wan day, but I'll no' be here to see it, Magnus and nor will du."

Magnus laughed.

"No, I'll wager I won't."

Seemon thought of the others waiting to see Doull hang, and realised he'd put his foot in it.

"Na, Magnus, dat's no whit I meant," he said, but the damage had been done.

"I always kent I'd be back," said Magnus. "Once, we went up da Hwang Pu river ta Shanghai ta put off cargo. We were ashore for a night. Dis Cockney fellow I sailed wi', he said ta me ta come wi' him. I'd never been in port dere afore, so I did. He took me to a brothel, somewhere off da Great Western Road. Man dat wis a place! Pretty young things dat looked no more dan bairns. Dey'd do onything, man," he smiled, thinking back.

"Dis fellow, I'm damned if I can mind his name, I'd have been twenty at da time, he wis sharp to everything dat went on. He spoke to wan o' da girls in der own language, and she brought wis dis pipe. A great ornate thing, shaped like a snake. He said it was opium. I wisna sure, but he said it would do me no harm. We smoked and we smoked at it, passing it a'tween wis. I wis sick, but it wisna ill. Everything aboot me looked beautiful. No different dan afore, but I saw hit differently. Hours passed. Da feeling grew stronger and stronger, till I seemed to lose all idea of reality. Things began to appear in my head, Lord kens fae whar. And dan when I looked at da pipe, it had become a snake. I was frozen where I sat. It wriggled right up ower me, coiling itsel' around aboot me, as if it was a hoor seducing me. Dan afore I kent it, it wis aroond my neck, and tightening. It turned into a noose. A hangman's noose . . . "

He threw the rum down his throat.

"You see, I always kent I'd be back. Mind Haakie, da gold sovereign?"

Haakie nodded, touched by this memory. Both he and Seemon glared at each other. This talk was making their task still more unpleasant.

"Magnus, I'm sorry," said Seemon. "I reckon du'd be no an ill crater, gien da chance."

A sense of doom descended on the room. The stink of death seemed to cling to the air.

Suddenly Seemon got up. He went behind the bar, picked up the glass which Haakie had concealed and threw it onto the stone floor where it smashed into a million pieces. Then he went to the customer's side, took the glass that Mangus had emptied, and did the same.

"Go home, Magnus," he said, with an air of authority firm in this voice. It was a tone he seldom used.

Magnus looked at him, tired and worn out, a picture of dejection. The fight was gone from him.

He stood up to obey, and his foot crunched the glass on the floor. In a daze, he looked at Haakie and asked if he had done it.

"No," replied the proprietor, "It wis another hooligan dat should a' kent better."

"I'll no' be a party to dis. I tink da man's ill" hissed Seemon.

Haakie shrugged.

"I wanted nothing to do wi' it fae da start."

Magnus staggered to the door. Haakie had locked it.

"I'm going. Open it please, Haakie."

The unexpected burst the door down for him. Magnus sprawled on the floor. And there before him stood the factor, with a gang of rancelmen.

"So I've caught up wi' dee at last, Magnus Doull. I've been to Turmtillen but dere's none dere but dee old witch of a midder."

"Take him boys!"

One of the rancelmen tied his hands, with a tight thin cord. They marched him out of the alehouse. There was no fight left in him. He was like clay to be moulded and shaped in their hands.

The crowd jeered as they brought him out. Someone threw a stone.

"Murderer!" It was Isabella.

"I'd like to kill him mysel' "

She ran up to him, her hair freed from it's tight bun, her eyes like a she-cat's. It was all out in the open now, even her madness.

Isabella's prim bearing had exploded into embittered fanaticism.

She tried to scratch his face as they dragged him away. One of the men shouted at her to stay out of it.

"I canna. Da Loard's chosen me," she screamed at him, her reason finally consumed with hatred.

"Weel da Laird's chosen me, woman," shouted the factor.

They took Magnus to an empty shed by the Haa House, which was to act as a jail. He was thrown inside, into the darkness, and he heard the bolt slide shut on the door. Voices muttered and mumbled. He heard the high pitched squeal of Isabella Agnes Pole, begging to be the one to put the rope around his neck.

"They'll be no hanging till he's been tried," said the factor, but in a way that showed Magnus the kind of trial he could expect.

Then another voice began. It was More, the special constable. He spoke in a low voice that Magnus could not hear clearly.

He caught a word here a phrase there.

"You can't do this. I'm the representative of the law . . . my responsibility . . . "

"Stay out of it . . . " he heard the factor advise.

" . . . be forced to report . . . "

"No, you won't."

This Magnus heard. The factor left with the policeman.

Incarcerated in his makeshift prison, he felt as if the past was finally upon him. Wasn't it this and this alone he had returned for? To see it all done with, to take it to its conclusion?

He sat down upon the earthen floor. It was wet, and he stood up again. He peered about him in the gloom, trying to adjust his eyes to the change of light. He found a wooden bucket which provided him with a seat. The stupor of a few minutes ago left him. His mind became as clear as it had ever been. The whole of his life suddenly fitted together into a pattern. Objects and events that had hitherto seemed meaningless now assumed their true signifigance.

With an effort, he forced himself back through his memory. There were no hidden corners. Things that had been long forgotten became vivid and sharp. Impressions that had been the root cause of later actions linked together with their offspring.

He spoke his own name . . .

"Magnus Doull."

He said it again.

"Magnus Doull."

These sounds that were called words, what right had they to claim his identity? Was he not worth more than three syllables? Was not his persona as wide and complex as the universe? Words eloquent and abstract clouded over the brief clarity of thought. A moment of true elation passed away. In that second he grasped the truth of his own identity, all that composed he the creature.

Special Constable More patted the pocket of his well-tailored jacket. The factor was a fair man, he thought, enjoying the feel of the notes in his pocket. It wouldn't be necessary to make a report. After all, Doull was guilty. Everyone knew that.

He began packing his suitcase. There was no point in his waiting a week for the next steamer. Things here had been soured a bit, and he could now afford to hire a man to drive him by carriage overland to Lerwick.

His only regret was the fact that he had not been able to use his magic box of detective methods. But maybe the old fisherman was right about fingerprinting. Maybe it was a ridiculous idea, fated to be forgotten once the novelty had worn off.

He put the box in his case.

"I'll stay for the hanging," he thought. "I'll enjoy that."

Chapter Twenty-Two

The Final Outcome

Isabella Agnes went back to her house.

Magnus Doull was at last to be brought to justice!

Her wiry body twitched excitedly.

She couldn't sit. She paced the room.

Wind whistled outside. Dusk was falling over Mirkwick. She couldn't get him out of her brain.

There he was, only a hundred yards away, locked in a shed like an animal awaiting slaughter. Nervously, she began to tidy her hair, but lost interest.

She scratched her scalp.

She went to the fire which was on the point of going out, and gazed dreamily into it as she poked among it with an iron-rod.

The wind whistled in her ears.

"Burn him Isabella. Burn him. Witches should be burned."

She looked all about her. Where had the voice come from? Nothing. Was this the sign she had prayed for?

The voice of her long dead husband whispered in her ear.

"Burn him Isabella, he's a witch."

"Witches should be burned not hanged."

She sank to her knees.

"Oh Loard God, is dis whit I most dö?"

Again the voice of Tammas Pole echoed from beyond the great divide.

"Witches should be burned not hanged."

In Turmtillen, Meenie raked the fire.

Magnus had not come back.

She stared into the glowing embers.

"Fire!"

It was the fire!

She ran to the door and raced down the hill towards the pierhead. It might already be too late.

The pattern fitted now. She understood.

The new wooden door Magnus had made that summer swung open behind her. It creaked as it did so. The hinge needed oil.

In the Haa House, Lady Isobelle and Ellen Mitchell sat in front of a huge fire in the drawing room.

Together they had prayed for the soul of Magnus Doull, ever since the girl's vision in the Kirk.

It seemed all they could do.

Ellen's eyes were fixed on the flame.

Suddenly she screamed, a terrifying shriek which pierced the quiet and brought the servants running.

"I saw him," she sobbed, "I saw him in the fire."

In the dark windy night, Isabella stood watching as the flames grew on the straw roofed shed.

Her eyes gleamed with the reflection of the yellow tongues. Wind acted as bellows, puffing and gusting at the fire.

It caught light quickly, smoking a lot at first, but slowly the intensity of the heat forced her farther and farther away.

She threw the rest of the oil-soaked rags onto the roof

of the shed. It was time to disappear. Let them think it was the Hand of the Lord.

Magnus awoke coughing. The shed was full of smoke. The roof was on fire! Adrenalin shot into his arms and legs; he bounded to the door and began beating on it.

It was heavy wood that enclosed him. The roar of the flames grew louder and louder. No one would hear his cries above that.

Meenie saw the flames as she ran towards the beach.

They leapt high into the black sky over Mirkwick, every second higher. Large balls of flame blew off the roof in the gale. She ran faster, breathing heavily through tired lungs. She came to the beach. The rock under her feet slowed her progress, so she went to the shoormil where it was sandy.

Water splashed up about her legs.

The beach seemed longer than ever before. Breaths were gasped shorter, oxygen harder to come by. Her old legs became jelly.

A pain swelled in her chest.

The cold sea air, smell of tang, water over her wirsit socks, and smooth sand under her feet.

The pain in her heart.

Her heart!

She slumped to the sand, falling in the shallow water. The sea blew waves across her heaving body. She saw stars in the sky high above, twinkling like beacons off then on.

A bird swept by. She tried to move to see what it was, but couldn't. Again it passed her swooping low. She caught sight of it. It was the rook.

And she knew who the fool had been.!

The cards had foretold her *own* death, and she had been too blind to understand.

Seaweed decorated her soaking body.

The tide, ever in motion, licked her face.

A crowd had gathered at the fire. They stood, unable to do anything as it spread to surrounding buildings. Other sheds began to burn as balls of flaming straw were sent flying through the air by the wind, setting light to any flammable substance they met with.

They had to evacuate the Haa. It seemed the safest thing to do, considering the wind direction.

The laird's household stood on the other side of the cobbled street from the villagers, ill at ease, having been brought to their level.

The laird himself stomped about anxiously. He ordered a hose to be fixed to the water pump, and played on the Haa side next the fire, in order to stop it igniting.

Mrs Williamson offered the hospitality of her house to the womenfolk from the big house. They accepted.

It took a long time for the fire to die down. The Haa itself was spared, though it took a terrible roasting, and the rooms smelled with smoke for long to come.

"It wis da Hand o' da Loard," proclaimed Isabella, her eyes glinting with satisfaction.

Folk turned to look at her.

She said no more.

Everyone agreed it was a poor end, even for a murderer, to be burnt alive. No one was happy about it. Except Isabella.

Haakie Manson put the bolt on the alehouse door.

The stink of the smoke was everywhere. He looked at the ship's clock above the bar. It was three o'clock. He yawned.

It was done. Finished with.

"Haakie," croaked a voice.

The publican jolted his head to a shadowed corner.

It was him.

"Magnus!"

"Thought I'd had it eh? So did I."

Magnus emerged from the shadow. The glow of the fire still alive lit his profile.

"But how, Magnus?"

The red-haired sailor flopped into a seat.

"A huge section of thatchin' fell into da shed. I had to get out. Though it hurt me."

He held up his hands, horribly burned and blistered.

"But I don't feel pain, do I Haakie? I've endured it for so lang."

Suddenly Magnus rose from the seat. He sprang forward and grabbed the publican by the neck.

"Magnus! I canna breathe."

Magnus rammed the barrel of the policeman's missing pistol into the fat landlord's spine.

"I did some thinkin' Haakie. I was crazy not to think o' it afore," he spat.

Haakie tried to swallow.

"Du's chokin' me."

"I ken," said Magnus, his fearsome gaze burning blue under his forehead. "Why, Haakie, why wis du so keen to help me escape ten years ago? Why? Dat's whit I kept asking mysel'. It's simple, isn't it? I was crazy not to realise da wan man dat wid ken da whole story. Du kept on sayin' . . . 'Dey'll hang dee, Magnus,' as du rowed. Why Haakie? Whit wis it du wis coverin' up?"

Haakie hissed. "Du's crazy."

"No man, I was crazy not to realise."

He shoved the gun into the publican's back again.

"And noo I want da whole story."

His grip closed tight around the fat throat.

"I canna tell dee. Kill me, for I'll die anyway."

Magnus swore at him.

"Damn dee, I'm a murderer. I'll kill dee all right."

"Du's no murderer, Magnus. Du doesna have da guts. Du couldna kill ten years ago no more dan du could noo," hissed Haakie.

Magnus let the man go.

"So it wisna me!" he exclaimed incredulously. "After all dis time, it wisna me."

Haakie looked at him angrily, rubbing his neck.

"Coorse it wisna dee. Du wis a drunk ten years ago, a drunk wi' a temper, but du wis never a murderer. Du wis just a perfect fool to take da blame. Dey'd a hanged dee, Magnus, if it hadna been for me. No, I said, let him go. He'll never come back as long as he believes dere's a noose awaiting him."

Magnus looked at him.

"Wha's 'dey', Haakie?" He levelled the gun at him.

"Magnus, kill me if du must, but I can never tell. Dere's folk involved dat wid see me dead if I spoke da truth. Besides, I only ken da half o' it. Dere's things dat happen here dat even I don't ken aboot. But for now, things should be left as dey are. As far as folk are concerned, da murderer's dead. It's all cleared up."

"I want da truth, Haakie."

"Kill me dan. Make deesel a murderer after all, and spend da rest o' dy life wi' dy conscience. Can't du see, du's free noo, *free* Magnus?"

Magnus dropped the gun at his feet.

"Ten years ago du helped me escape. Can du do da same again?"

Haakie nodded.

He went behind the bar, took a piece of paper and a pen, and wrote a short letter which he handed to Magnus.

"I can't take da boat oot da night. But take dis note, and go to my cousin in Scalloway. Go right away. He'll pit dee up, until du can get aff da island. And Magnus, dis time, don't come back!"

And into Magnus' hand he pressed a single gold sovereign.

Chapter Twenty Three

Pexins

Aa'body agreed they had never seen the like of it. Meenie Doull lying dead in the tide, and Magnus her murderous son burnt alive in his prison. The Lord had certainly taken his revenge on them.

Haakie Manson poured two glasses of rum from the bottle. He handed one to Seemon, who was filling his pipe at the other side of the bar.

"I hear we're to have a new laird," said Seemon.

"Aye" said Haakie.

"An yon policeman fellow's awa' ."

"Aye," replied Haakie.

"It's been a bad business right fae da start."

"Aye," said Haakie.

Seemon lit his pipe.

"Still, it's aa' resolved noo, thank da Loard. I winder whit dis new Laird'll be like?"

Haakie sipped his rum.

"I heard he'll no' be livin' here. He'll have a man to manage da estate, and just visit noo and again to see it's all in order. Well, it's nearly da end o' anidder year, Haakie. It seems to have been a lang wan."

Glasses emptied.

Haakie refilled them.

"An' whit aboot yon young Jacobsen boy elopin' wi' Agnes Williamson of da shop-? Yon wis a surprise . . ." Seemon went on.

"Aye."

"Haakie, du's no desel. Time wis I could hold a good conversation wi' dee, but noo it's aa' just yes and no."

"It's better no' to get involved in ither folk's business. Dat's whit I believe, Seemon."

The old fishermen spluttered his rum over the counter.

"Come on noo Haakie, did I hear dee right?"

Magnus Doull, beard shaved off, hair cut short, hands heavily bandaged climbed the gangway to the Nort' o' Scotlan' boat to Leith.

In his old canvas kitbag, he still had quite a bit of his savings. He watched a young couple sitting opposite him, and could have sworn he recognised them. Wasn't she the daughter of Robert o' da shop in Mirkwick? And he the young fellow that had worked there?

He eavesdropped on their conversation.

"Peter," she said, "I can't help feeling what we did was wrong."

"Agnes, Agnes. Du said deesel dat we couldna wait forever. And after all, da money wis dine in a way. Didn't he say that you'd have it shared a'tween you when you married?"

"Yes, I know . . . "

She smiled at him with blind unseeing love.

"It was an awful clever plan, to put the blame on those sailors. You're so clever, Peter," she crooned admiringly.

"And dee, Agnes, whit a part du played wi' dy faint. Du should be on da stage."

"Maybe I will be, one day, in New Zealand," she giggled.

He leant across, and kissed her on the nose.

"Mr and Mrs Peter Jacobsen," she sighed. "I can hardly believe it!"

Magnus smiled. He rose up and went out on deck. The steamer was passing the entrance to Lerwick harbour. He looked long and hard at the outline of the town against the hills and sky behind. To the east, the islands of Bressay and Noss rose sheer out of the sea. He would not be back. He knew that.

New Zealand. Now there was a thought. It was a new land, where a man could build a good life for himself. It was still a challenge, untamed. Maybe there he would find what he sought.

He watched the south mainland slide past and away, into the distance. Here and there he could see houses, scattered.

What would become of this place? What did the fates have in store for it?

He tried to imagine it at the end of another century. Would the peat fires still burn, would the boats still lie in their noosts? Would there ever be a time when these Northern islands blossomed, their long winter ended? He would have loved to have stayed to find out, but he knew that it was against his nature. This exile that awaited him, this was his pexins.

He rummaged in the old kit-bag. There in the corner he found it; his hand caressed its rough texture. He put it to his lips, smelled its peculiar aroma. Then he carefully replaced it in his bag.

A tiny clod of peat.